I0630919

BOOK ONE OF THE
CLAN NOVEL:TREMERE TRILOGY

By Eric Griffin

To Jennifer,
Memories of childhood,
Visions of beauty,
All too soon to pass by.

"And even in our sleep pain that cannot forget falls drop by drop upon the heart, and in our own despair, against our will, comes wisdom to us by the aweful grace of God."

—Aeschylus

Chapter 1
Les Tremeres

Antigone Baines awoke with a start, too frightened to move. Her limbs were as stiff as those of a corpse. They trembled slightly as if disturbed by the vibration of footsteps overhead — a stranger walking upon her grave.

The unsettling image was perhaps a shade too close to the truth. With a shudder, she forced it from her mind and pressed her body back down into the wrinkled bedclothes that still unmistakably bore the outline of her slumbering form. As if she might sink from sight altogether. To lie unnoticed. Forgotten.

There was a solace in being unnoticed. It was an art that Antigone had long cultivated. There was a face she presented to the world—the face of a young woman of no more than twenty-eight years. But even she had to admit to herself that it was no more real than the grainy, yellowed photographs relegated to the very last pages of the family album. It might have been her own face once, years ago. But if it were, there was no way to prove it now. And if it were not, there was no one left who might accuse her or say how she might have come by it.

It was a pleasant enough face. Smiling. Some would say pretty. But it wasn't a face you could look at without wondering. Wondering at the lack of color (as in an old photograph) in the youthful cheeks. Or at the eyes. They were *old* eyes, there was no other way of describing them. Not old like grandmother-eyes, with the skin pinched up around the edges like piecrust. Old like the eyes of serpents are old. Seeing back to the beginnings of things.

Antigone lay very still, alone in the cocoon of darkness. There was no hammering of blood in her ears, no racing of her heart to intrude upon the absolute silence. She strained to pick out the sound of the stranger's breathing.

Nothing.

Her body was bathed in blood-sweat. Her hands were clammy with the sweet, sticky vitae. The satiny sheets were already ruined.

She forced herself to calm, but those eyes—those serpent's eyes—they kept rigidly open, unblinking. They refused to close again upon nightmare; they refused to pick out any details of the shadowy objects in the room. To give them form was, in some inexplicable way, to give them life.

It was some time before she could convince herself that she was safe, within the familiar confines of the novice *domicilium*. A nightmare, nothing more. For the third night in a row, Antigone had dreamt of the Children Down the Well.

It was always the same—the faces of the children peering up at her from their watery tomb. Antigone could find no hint of accusation in their glassy, unblinking eyes, nor words of condemnation on their cold, bluish lips. But the very sight of them sufficed to fill her with unreasoning dread.

Their eyes entreated her, pleaded with her. But their blue-tinged lips could give no voice to their desperate need. She could never wrest from them the secret of what it was they expected of her.

Antigone steeled her resolve and allowed her eyelids to droop slightly. She knew that the faces would be there still, awaiting her return. Round and bright as moons, smiling up at her from just beneath the surface of the still water. Infinitely patient.

Only they were not there. No children, no well. Only darkness awaited her, damning in its mundanity. Much to her dismay, Antigone realized that the Children's sudden absence was more ominous even than their presence.

Where was the young girl of five years that was always the first to pluck (with pudgy blue fingers) at the hem of Antigone's robes? In her mind, she could see the girl still, could trace the gentle curve of her smooth, unblemished cheek. The child's green eyes were as large and perfectly round as saucers. Her long black hair fanned out all around the bright face like a fishing net cast out upon the surface of the dark waters. Tangled strands lapped gently at the slick side of the well. But now, she was gone.

The faces had never moved nor spoken before. Although they were calm, almost serene, Antigone knew that their deaths had not been quiet ones. They had been drowned, all of them. Cast into the well, abandoned to panic, flounder and sink beneath the chill waters. Lost to sight. Lost to memory.

If only they would stay down.

Antigone had always suspected that the well was secretly brimming full of youth, swarming with bright, golden eyes, buoyed up ever nearer to the well's lip by the sheer press of bodies beneath. She had always imagined that some night soon she might awake to find that they had spilled out over the brink of the well—crossing the line into the waking world. It was not a comforting thought.

Antigone did not fear death. It was something of a childhood companion of hers. She could remember no fewer than six distinct encounters with death. Seven separate lifetimes. It was easy, really, once you knew how. The trick was in the names. There was a magic in names.

The earliest one that she could recall was Antigone Ruth Scoville, but there was no telling how many more might have slipped past her before she had caught on to how the game was

4 / Eric Griffin

played. Years later she would go back and recheck the birth records at the Scoville Congregationalist Church in Scoville, Massachusetts, and find that one Antigone Ruth was born to Captain and Mrs. James Scoville on the twenty-first day of February in the year of Our Lord nineteen hundred and one.

02/21/1901. Zero plus two, plus two plus one, plus one plus nine plus zero plus one equals sixteen. One plus six equals seven. It was her grandmother (on her mother's side) who had first pointed out that seven was a very important number for Antigone. A magical number. That much had stuck with her.

She repeated the comforting numerology like a mantra. It helped her fend off the yawning chasm of dread that was opening within her. She did not fear her own death, but she did fear the Children, their expectation, their all-consuming need. And she feared that, once again, she would be unable to help them.

From somewhere close at hand, Antigone's straining ears picked out a mournful sound. A single rasping sob. Then the silence settled over her once again.

Only one of the other of the novices, she thought. But the sound was enough. It broke the spell the Children had cast over her. The rigid paralysis. It gave her something to focus on. She swung her feet out over the edge of the bed before she had a chance to change her mind.

Antigone slid her robe over her head in one fluid shrug. Her bare feet squelched slightly on the cool, tiled floor. After a few steps, the trail of bloody footprints became nothing more than indistinct red smudges as she padded quietly out of the door of the *domicilium.* Her feet carried her instinctively along the familiar path down toward the chantry's security-control room.

Already, the intensity of the night tremors—*les tremeres*— had lost its hold upon her. With each step, she grew more alert, poised, professional, deadly. By the time she reached the control room, there was little trace of the frightened novice about her. She had donned her death mask, crafted herself into a veritable visitation from the grave.

Chapter 2
A Protective Circle, Inverted

"I came as soon as I heard. I…" Antigone broke off, cursing softly. "What the hell happened here?"

Antigone liked to think of herself as a seasoned veteran, a veteran of many lifetimes. Someone who was not easily or unduly alarmed. She prided herself on her ability to draw a sharp line between the utter helplessness of the night tremors and the cool efficiency with which she faced the waking nightmare.

But what she saw here frightened her.

Helena did not glance up from where she knelt over the body of Aisling Sturbridge, the regent of the Chantry of Five Boroughs. The three women were deep within the catacombs beneath the chantry house, surrounded by shards of masonry from the shattered crypts. Sturbridge curled in upon herself, all sharp angles, elbows and knees. Her robes were soaked with icy water. Against one wall of the rough-hewn chamber were the remains of a diagramma hermetica.

"I'm not sure what happened," Helena said. "This is how I found her, and she hasn't stirred since. I don't think she's lost to us yet, but she's certainly not *here* anymore. I was afraid to try to move her. I had just about resigned myself to the thought of having to keep a solitary vigil here until sundown. What were you doing up and monitoring the chantry security channels at this hour?"

"Couldn't sleep," Antigone said.

At this statement, Helena turned and gave the novice a hard look. Among the living, going without food or sleep might be an option. Among their kind, however, there were fewer choices. The primal desires had a way of asserting themselves, of taking the bit in the teeth. And they brooked little dissention. When the sun rose, it forced the body down into a fitful slumber from which only the sun's setting would release it again. The sleep of the dead. When the inner Beast hungered, you arose, you hunted, you fed.

If you were smart, you didn't press the issue. You didn't ask too many questions. You didn't test just how far you could stretch the tether. As head of chantry security, Helena had, on more than one occasion, had the unpleasant responsibility of having to 'put down' a novice who made the mistake of thinking she could ignore the dictates of the Beast. The results were never pretty.

"It must be nice," Helena said dismissively and returned her attention to her patient.

Antigone fidgeted. "I mean, I was awakened. It was nothing. Just a...dream." Confused and embarrassed, she stumbled over the words.

"A nightmare?" Helena asked. The strain in her voice was barely perceptible. To any other ear, it would have sounded calm, level, tightly controlled.

"No," Antigone replied a bit too quickly. She would not have the adepta thinking her some frightened child. Then she considered further. "Actually, no. It *wasn't* a nightmare. I can't remember very much of what it was at all. But why should a dream wake me at all, much less so if it wasn't even a nightmare? Oh, never mind. You must think me very silly already."

"Not at all," Helena replied. "There's nothing silly about them. The nightmares, I mean. *Les tremeres.*"

"You have them too," Antigone accused, realization slowly dawning. "You couldn't sleep either. That's why you were wandering around down here." She shivered. Her voice dropped to a conspiratorial whisper. "You have seen them, in your dreams. The Children Down the Well." She could see them before her eyes even now. Their hair spread out like seaweed upon the dark waters. Their serene blue faces bobbing against the slick stones. Their eyes wide and bright as moons.

Helena did not answer her right away. "It wasn't the Children who woke me," she replied at last, a grudging admission. "It was more like their sudden absence. The fact that they were no longer there, anywhere. I searched for them, but I couldn't find them."

"You *looked* for them, Adepta?" Antigone asked incredulously. "Jeez, most nights I would be thrilled if they just left me alone for a..." She broke off. If she would be thrilled, then why had she awakened bolt upright in a blood-sweat?

"When you woke up," Helena asked cautiously, "was anything...wrong?"

Antigone started as if the adepta had read her thoughts. Not in surprise, but in resentment at the perceived intrusion. There were always whispers among the novices, of course, that certain of their instructors had actually mastered the power of reading minds. Antigone had been at the chantry long enough to guard jealously what little privacy was allotted to her—even if it were only the privacy of her own thoughts. "How do you mean, wrong?"

"Were you hurt?" Helena asked.

"No, of course not. I woke up in a sweat. The sheets are ruined, I'm afraid, but other than that, no. Why do you ask?" Antigone realized the answer to her question as soon as she asked it and she knelt down next to the adepta in concern. She hesitated, caught between laying a hand reassuringly on

Helena's arm and the reproach that such familiarity might invoke. "Are you all right?" she asked in a whisper.

Helena nodded but her face was grim and drawn. It had been hours, and she was certain the bleeding had not yet abated. It was, perhaps, too cruel and intimate a reminder of what she had sacrificed in joining the ranks of the Tremere.

"Whatever has happened," Helena said, "the Children are gone. Sturbridge is nearly dead. I awake to find myself...injured. And you startle awake sweating blood. Someone's got to check on the others."

"I'll stay with the regentia. You go. We'll be fine," she added, sensing Helena's reluctance.

Helena stiffened. "I'm not leaving her. Not until I find out what happened here. You go up and see to the others. There may be other casualties."

Antigone stared at her superior in open concern. Helena's hurt must have been much deeper than she was admitting. What had been done to her?

"The others," Antigone repeated hollowly. Then she seemed to come to back to herself. "Any sign of our other missing persons? The security-systems daemon is still reporting the ambassador and Eva as missing in action."

"Signs, yes. But not promising ones. There's a heap of ash at the bottom of that central well that's fresh enough that it still holds the shape of a man." *But only just barely*, Helena thought. She knew that if she were to touch it, or even brush too close to it, the whole fragile construct would collapse under its own weight and scatter.

"The ambassador, Adepta?" Antigone asked. "I must have walked right past him in the dark on the way down."

"Consider yourself lucky not to have ended up lying *beside* him. It's all too easy to take a misstep in the dark down here. That was one of the first things I did when I took over as head of chantry security—make sure this whole damned area was strictly off limits. Except for formal funerary functions. But if I had my way, we wouldn't even use it for that. I'd be just as happy to brick the whole thing up and forget about it."

"Tell me about it," Antigone said. "The whole way down here I kept thinking that this maze of crypts was contrived just to pitch you over the edge of that central courtyard. There are a couple of exposed stretches on the way down where it's easier to lose the path than to keep to it."

Helena shook her head. "That's actually not far from the truth. Some of the deadfalls were designed precisely to dispose of unwanted persons—or at least the remains of unwanted persons. Talbott says that at least one early regent so hated the very thought of coming down here that she ordered her novices to sweep the ash and bone from the upper crypts down into the central well. To make room for more interments in the uppermost galleries. A charming custom don't you think?"

Ashes down the well, Antigone thought. "Delightful. But you said you had found 'signs,' plural. Any trace of Eva?"

Helena turned slowly and Antigone followed the adepta's gaze to the center of the room. There, on the floor, an outline like a shadow was seared into the very stone. But it was a shadow in photo negative—the blazing white shape of a young woman, her arms thrown up protectively before her face.

Antigone whistled low. "You call that 'not promising'? I'd hate to see a sign that you'd call grim."

"Sturbridge's condition is grim," Helena said flatly. "I fear we may lose her. I cannot let that happen."

That pronouncement knocked all trace of levity out of Antigone. She reached out to brush the face of the fallen regent with her fingertips. It was chill to the touch. Antigone thought she could detect a bluish tinge to Sturbridge's features. The regent's wet and matted hair fanned wildly about her like a shattered halo, as if she had been thrown violently to the ground. Antigone unconsciously began to smooth the hair back into place. "Can we move her?"

Helena scowled down at the novice as if she might rebuke her for the presumption of daring to touch the regent's body. But the adepta held her peace. "I wouldn't want to risk lifting her, if that's what you mean. Nothing seems to be broken, but she might well be paralyzed for all she's stirred since I've found her."

"Could we try an apportation?" Antigone asked. "That might at least get her out of this place—off the stone floor and back to her sanctum. Into her own bed. It's damp down here and the air..." She shuddered.

Helena, resigned, nodded her assent. "All right. It's worth a try. There are chalk and candles over there, by the *diagramma*. But be careful. We'll have to improvise a bit and just draw the circle around her where she lies."

Antigone arose slowly, feeling some hint of Helena's reluctance to leave Sturbridge's side. She crossed the room toward the remains of the mystic diagram. "Do you think the link would be more stable if we channeled it through this existing—" She broke off. "Um, Helena? Have you seen this diagram over here?"

"I have," Helena replied and left it at that.

Not the most helpful of answers, Antigone thought. What the hell was this thing? She made a complete circuit of the diagram. "This doesn't make any sense," she called, realizing a hint of her apprehension had crept into her voice. "The wardings are all wrong. It looks like they're pointing inward. Why would you draw a protective circle that's all *inverted* like this?"

Helena did not answer right away. Then, "My first thought was that it was some kind of prison," she replied. "But for whom? Or perhaps the question is, for what? Maybe you summon something *into* it. Something you might want to talk to, but that you definitely would not want getting any better foothold into this world…."

Antigone frowned and considered. "If it is, it's the damnedest spirit cage I've ever come across. Why would you need to protect the entity you've summoned? Unless the very climate of this world could harm it. Like conjuring you or me out into a sunny meadow."

"I said that was my *first* impression. But if you can come up with the diagram that can protect against *that*, they'll give you your own chantry."

Antigone flushed bright red. Helena's rebuke had hit a sore spot and she was well aware of it. The enigmatic 'they'—the Tremere hierarchy. The Pyramid. There was simply no way the Tremere powers-that-be would ever give Antigone her own chantry. And she and Helena both knew it. Twice now they had flatly denied her promotion past the first circle of the novitiate. And it wasn't her fault. None of this was her fault.

Seventy years, she thought. After seventy years of service—of *exemplary* service—it still didn't matter. Antigone was unpromotable. And she was likely to stay that way, indefinitely.

They said in Scoville that the Sight—and the gifts that accompany it—always runs in the female line. But if that were true, it ran right past Antigone. Medea, her younger sister, could tell you when a storm was coming and was handy with a hex or a potion. Dispensing warts and love philters, that sort of thing. Her older sister, Electra—well, Electra's enchantments were less arcane and more efficacious than any love philter. An enviable combination of charm, beauty, and the promise of property. But she came by them all honestly—her beauty from mother, the property from father, and charm from Miss Jane Simpson's Academie for Girls. You really couldn't fault her for it. She was easily the most gifted of the three sisters. And everyone in town knew it. Including Electra. They could hardly have kept such a thing from her.

But Antigone was hopeless. If there were a magic bone in her body, it was buried deep. Deep enough that even now—almost one hundred years later—she still defied the best efforts of several master thaumaturges to try to teach her any more than the bare rudiments of the blood arts. The theory she understood in excruciating detail, but the practice...

She had only ever known that one trick: her deadly game of ledges. The intricate dance along the threshold between life and death. She could remember the first time she had pulled it off, the precise morning: February 7th, 1906. It was exactly two weeks before her fifth birthday. The day was another perfect seven, although she did not realize this until years later. It wasn't really the numbers that were important, after all. It was the names.

On that morning she descended to breakfast rather abruptly, by means of the most direct and precipitous route possible—through the French doors of her parents' second-story bedroom. Out onto the widow's walk and over the railing.

When she regained consciousness later that afternoon, she was back in her own bed. The doctor had banished everyone but her mother from the room. Antigone heard them talking in hushed tones about fractures and concussions, but could not imagine what they meant by either their words or their solemnity. She had won! Didn't they understand that?

It didn't matter, they would see in time. They would all see. There would be plenty of time, now. All of time, in fact.

Antigone shivered involuntarily. The clammy air of the crypts seemed to grope at her. She tried to concentrate on the intricacies of the diagram. Sturbridge's death must be hovering very close now. Antigone could almost hear the buffeting of black wings drawing closer in ever-tightening gyres. She forced her attentions back to the wardings and blurted out the first words that came into her head. "There are none of the standard glyphs for elemental forces that you would need to bridge to such an alien world. No, I don't think it can be a prison. Could this be part of some exorcism rite?"

"Hmm. I hadn't thought about it," Helena replied. "You mean like trying to protect someone possessed from something that was already inside him? I'm not sure that would really work, but it's a bit outside of my field. I wouldn't want to have to say for certain one way or the other. But I believe we're missing some of the standard 'bell, book and candle' trappings. That and the fact that I think these things usually require a priest of some sort...."

Antigone was flustered now. "Yes, yes. I see your point. And getting a priest down here—to participate in some hermetic vampiric blood rite, no less—would be a dubious proposition at best. I can't even imagine why the regentia would be down here. Much less with Eva and the ambassador."

"That's been bothering me as well," Helena admitted. "Of the three, only Sturbridge should have been able to access the crypts. I can't think that she'd just decide to bring a novice and a visiting dignitary down here on a whim. And she and the ambassador were never what I'd call close."

"They fought like wolves, if that's what you mean," Antigone said.

"The regentia was always the very image of the polite hostess," Helena said pointedly. "She was precisely polite. I would be very careful how I characterized her relationship with the ambassador, if I were you. Especially given the current *unpleasantries*. There are certain to be inquiries. Inquiries I would not like to find myself on the receiving end of."

Antigone's eyes widened. "I didn't mean—you don't think—"

"It's all right. Your words will remain between us. Let us hope, however, that the regentia recovers before the

Fatherhouse in Vienna turns up the pressure. I'm sure there are perfectly reasonable answers to what transpired here. But unfortunately for us, they are all currently locked up within the regentia's head. If we should lose her now..."

Helena didn't need to spell it out for her. *If we should lose her now*, Antigone thought, *then we're on our own when the special ops from Vienna arrive.*

Antigone had never seen the Astors in action, but there wasn't a chantry security officer anywhere who hadn't heard the stories. What they had done to the chantry house in Tel Aviv was only their most recent—and most ruthless—'liquidation.'

The M.O. was always the same. They came in hard and fast. They shut the place down to stop the spread of the contagion. Then they started probing, holding everything and everyone up against the yardstick of idealized party standards. They rooted out the canker at its source and they weren't too concerned in what they had to cut through to get to it. But they got the job done, and by the end of the whirlwind field surgery, Vienna would have its exemplary local chantry back in working order.

Antigone knew that a visit from the Astors now would mean that both she and Helena were out of job. Within the Tremere Pyramid, there was little ambiguity about the term 'termination.' And the less talk of 'severance' that went along with it, the better. Antigone doubted if even she could snatch her own death back from the hands of a determined inquisitor. She tried to recall the precise details surrounding each of her six transitions—the dramatic, almost staged, passages from one lifetime to the next. Had she ever been able to pull off the trick under duress? In the presence of witnesses?

Like a sleepwalker, Antigone crossed the crypt and, without a word, handed over the chalk and candles to Helena. She carried out the adepta's instructions deftly, but without any real conviction. Like a volunteer from the audience, unsure of exactly how the trick was performed.

Helena said nothing, but she must have repented of her earlier cruelty. She was painfully considerate of Antigone's limitations and did not ask the novice to assist in anything more rigorous than arranging the ceremonial props for the rite of apportation.

Antigone could only look on enviously as the adepta invoked the power of the blood. As she interwove the diverse elements of chalk and candlelight, arcane glyphs and sacred names. After seventy years of service to the Pyramid, Antigone still knew no more 'magic' than the lone trick she had carried with her since childhood—her theatrical disappearing act (now you see her, now you don't) between life and death.

She had hoped, in time, to find some way to win their grudging respect. When Helena had created the chantry's security team, Antigone was the first to volunteer for the dangerous and onerous duty. But that had not stemmed the whisperings.

She had heard them, of course. It would have been impossible to keep them hidden from her. And her fellow novices had little inclination to conceal their barbs. Jackal, they called her. Because that was her job. Pyramid security. Like Anubis—the laughing, jackal-headed warden of the dead—Antigone kept careful watch over the house of the undying.

"I'm taking her through now," Helena said. "You check on the others. And then try to get some rest. You look like hell."

"Thanks," Antigone muttered. "You could use a little beauty rest your—"

But they were already gone. Helena and Sturbridge had flickered once and vanished, leaving Antigone to find her own way out of the crypts.

Chapter 3
Drawing Down the Dragon

Ivory rattled in the darkness. *A sound like sifting old bones over a discarded window screen,* Felton thought. Except that here the stakes were far greater than the usual takings—the occasional gold filling or wedding band.

"East Wind." The voice cracked and sputtered, an abrasive sound like the striking of a match.

There was a collective murmur from the ring of conspirators, and the ivories danced once again. The sound drew closer. Felton tried to gauge how close. He could make out few details in the darkened interior. The only light in the room came from the sporadic flash of neon marquee through the slats of the blinds. Despite his most careful interrogation, the room stubbornly refused to surrender its secrets.

Under less trying circumstances, Felton knew enough that he might recognize two of his associates by sight, and he had ferreted out the names of two others. The rest of the Conventicle was known to him only by their hushed voices or by the outline of their shadowy presences. He guessed that there were maybe twelve of them here tonight. A bigger crowd than was usual. Felton disliked crowds almost as much as he disliked anything out of the ordinary—especially in such a delicate situation as this.

The conspirators sat in a rough circle, their high-backed chairs the only furnishings apparent in the theatre loft. Felton fidgeted, running his hands over the polished wood of the armrests. He could feel the weight of great age and craftsmanship there. No stage props, these. Idly, he picked at the orderly ranks of cool brass rivets that tacked down the upholstery. His hand instinctively shied away from making contact with the hide that covered the seat. Its touch reminded him of an old, shed snakeskin. It crackled unpleasantly each time Felton shifted in his seat.

The clattering of the ivories paused and the room again grew expectantly silent.

"South Wind." It was a different voice this time. Its disappointment was evident, but it was quickly drowned out beneath the renewed machine-gun rattle of the mingling bones.

"It is good to have you among us at last."

Felton barely caught the whispered welcome. The speaker evidently thought to conceal his words beneath the vigorous shaking of the ivories. Felton knew that words were not intended for him.

A man, who must have been seated a few places to his left, replied, "It was touch and go for a while there. I didn't know if we would be able to shake free of him. The entire city he is content to let fall into neglect and ruin, but us..."

"I know, I know. But we will speak no more of this tonight. You are here with us now and that is what matters."

Felton became aware of the steady, padded tread of footfalls approaching. The bones clattered to rest once more.

"North Wind." That was Charlie's voice, and there was an ill-disguised note of relief in it. So old Charlie had dodged the bullet. Probably just as well. If he were really any good at this covert stuff, he wouldn't have been the only one present whom Felton knew by name, face, and voice. Heck, he even knew where Charlie went to ground most mornings. Charlie was a good enough sort, but Felton shared his relief that the old man was well clear of this damned fool mission.

They were all damned fool missions these nights. It was different back when they were picking away at the Sabbat. Had it only been a few short weeks ago? It seemed like a mortal lifetime or more. Sure, the Sabbat would kill you as soon as look at you. But it was never a case of getting drafted to tackle some war pack head on. You reconnoitered. You disrupted supply and communications. If you saw a good clean shot, you took it (and those missions were always the sweetest). But you got in and out fast—before you accidentally developed any "lasting entanglements."

Now it was all different. If there were any Sabbat left, they had gone underground and were lying low, keeping out of sight. It wasn't something they were any good at, though. Once you'd been top dog in town for a while, you developed a little bit of a swagger. Felton could see it happening already, with the Camarilla 'liberators' and this new Provisional Council. It wouldn't be long before they were as bad, if not worse, than the damned Sabbat ever were. He guessed that's why he was still here, why their little knot of resistance was still together, still fighting. They couldn't let things get out of hand that way again.

That or we just couldn't stand to let it go. He looked around the circle of grim figures crouched in the silence of the darkened loft. Could they let it all go, and walk away? Could any of them? Could he?

Not for the first time, he found himself wondering what he would do if he weren't out there in the streets each night, fighting the good fight. He closed his eyes and let the ring of twelve figures surrounding him take on a very different aspect. They now surrounded a massive boardroom conference table. He pictured them all decked out in smart business suits, endlessly debating points of order and precedence; struggling to maintain the Traditions, the Masquerade. He tried to envision himself as a Camarilla power player: currying support, offering double-edged favors and swapping an ever-changing procession of pawns.

Yeah, right. Not him. This was all he knew anymore. The upper hand. The nightly struggle for dominance in the streets.

Something rattled like a snake right in front of his nose. He recoiled before he could catch himself.

"Easy now, hero," came the soft chiding voice. "One in twelve's not half bad odds. Nothing to shy away from." The speaker shook the bag vigorously.

Felton snorted his derision, a sound that cut clearly through the rattling of the bones. He grabbed the other's wrist and drew it closer, bearing down a few degrees harder than was necessary. His other hand found the open mouth of the coarse sacking.

"It's one in nine now, genius." He slipped his hand within and rummaged among the cool ivory of the mah-jongg tiles. He scooped them all up and allowed them to gradually sift through his fingers until there was only one left. He withdrew his clenched fist and blew on it for luck.

Slowly he uncoiled his fingers. He waited for the neon marquee outside to flash again, a knife-thrust of pink light slashing across the floorboards.

On the tile in his hand, Felton could pick out a delicate "S" etched in blue. It overlaid a compass rose whose downward spoke was highlighted with red. Another South Wind.

"Soap," he lied. "Blue Dragon. Looks like it's my lucky night."

He raised the tile and flashed the blank side around the room before stuffing it back into the sack. He knew that, in the darkness, they wouldn't be able to pick out the tile itself, much less the symbol inscribed upon it. But they would see the motion and that would be enough.

"You are a very fortunate man," purred the Bonespeaker, the sack of tiles dangling limp and forgotten from his hand, like a scythe in spring. "This mission will bring great glory to our cause. Your equipment and briefing are just outside the door. No one else will leave this room for another half an hour, so that there can be no risk that any here present might—inadvertently, of course—jeopardize your mission. We will not delay you further. Strike true."

Felton snorted. "Yeah, whatever. Just don't let me find you ladies waiting up for me when I get back, okay? I'd hate to think of anybody losing any sleep on my account."

They suffered his jibe in silence, each absorbed in his own private thoughts. But, as one, they all stood as he left the chamber—no one knowing with certainty if they would see him again.

Chapter 4
Eaters of the Dead

Sturbridge awoke, retching stagnant water. Her entire body heaved. She grasped at the bedcurtains to steady herself, but succeeded only in tearing away three of the rings that held them to the cast-iron canopy and falling heavily to the floor. Suddenly aware that she was not alone in the sanctum, she wiped at her mouth with the back of one hand with as much dignity as she could muster, and peered up miserably to meet the eyes of her guest.

"Helena," she managed to choke out, with apparent relief. "How long have…"

The adepta would not meet her regent's gaze. "I am pleased that you are among us again, Regentia. I feared for your life. You have been unconscious for the better part of a week."

"A week?" Sturbridge repeated hollowly, as if the words could find no purchase upon her thoughts. "An entire week, lost. My god, what have you told—"

"What could I tell them?" Helena interrupted with sudden vehemence. "I don't understand any of this. The prince is demanding to see you. Vienna wants to know why the ambassador hasn't reported in. And I'd like to know just what the hell is happening around here!"

Sturbridge, caught in a renewed fit of coughing, offered no answer. Concern was apparent on Helena's face, but still she hung back, making no move to approach or offer assistance. She tried to force her features into a mask of impassivity to cover the hint of rising panic stirring at the back of her mind. *Where is the blood?* As she gazed down at Sturbridge, that single thought kept nagging at her. Her kind drank blood, sweated blood, even cried blood. Sturbridge, however, continued to disgorge only stagnant water and gobbets of dead, bluish flesh. Helena turned away in revulsion. "Regentia, what has happened to the ambassador and to…Eva?"

At the note of horror and accusation in the adepta's voice, Sturbridge's head jerked up. She coughed and spat. "Oh, Helena. How could you think that I…" She rose staggeringly to her feet and reached out an unsteady hand toward the adepta.

Helena retreated stiffly. "What happened to them?" she repeated stubbornly.

Sturbridge leaned heavily against the bedpost. "This is not easy for me to say. I will understand if it is difficult for you to believe. Eva was responsible for the recent murders at the chantry. She lured the ambassador down to the crypts and killed him as well. You will find his remains at the bottom of the central well."

Helena nodded cautiously. That was exactly where she had found the ambassador's remains. "That's awfully convenient. The two of them going down into the crypts and killing each other, I mean."

Sturbridge regarded Helena quizzically, wondering at the hurt and bitterness in her voice. "The ambassador didn't kill Eva. I…I think I did."

Unseen, Helena's hands thrust down deep into the pockets of her robes and bundled into fists. One of them closed around something hard, smooth and wooden.

"What do you mean, 'you think'?" Helena's voice was icy.

Sturbridge could sense that the situation had taken an unpleasant turn. She was having trouble keeping herself upright and was concerned that the adepta could see how she sagged against the bedpost.

"Adepta. Helena. Sit down." Sturbridge gestured to a spot on the bed.

Helena's gaze was cold and distant, but she obeyed. "Yes, Regentia." She crossed the room and lowered herself into the indicated space. Sturbridge sank heavily down beside her.

"Helena, I cared for Eva very much, almost as if she were my own...child." Sturbridge choked on the word. "But that does not change the fact that I am responsible for the safety and well-being of this chantry. You understand that. I had to know what Eva was doing and why. I found out more than I wanted to know. Eva won't be hurting anybody anymore."

Helena's composure was obviously breaking. "Where is her body?" She pronounced each word separately and distinctly.

"It is burned, Helena. Consumed utterly. The light of truth is more ravenous even than sunlight."

The adepta thought of the stark white outline seared into the floor of the crypt where they had found Sturbridge. The regent's story could be construed as fitting with the evidence at the scene, as far as it went. Steeling herself, she turned and looked Sturbridge directly in the eye for the first time. There was no way to skirt the question delicately any longer.

"Regentia, there is evidence here that cannot be denied. You have been eating flesh. I put it to you that you have killed and devoured a novice entrusted to your care."

There, she had said it. The words sounded monstrous, almost ludicrous, on her lips. But there was no taking them back now.

Sturbridge looked both hurt and saddened. "No, Helena. Not in the way you mean, certainly. But they are all with me now. Within me. Eva, the ambassador, the Children..."

Sturbridge heard the distinctly animal cry break from Helena's throat and felt, rather than saw, the adepta's fist lash out. The blow caught her squarely in the chest and Sturbridge curled around it, doubling over. She gagged and felt the chill waters rising once again.

Tearing at the wooden shaft protruding from her chest, Sturbridge felt the waters of oblivion close over her head as she sank into the infinitely patient arms of the Children.

Chapter 5
An Elaborate Clockwork Toy

Emmett paused upon the threshold of the Chantry of Five Boroughs. He leaned heavily against the jamb as if gasping for breath — as if the strain of hauling his broken body the length of the entry hall had nearly proved too much for him. He drew a shuddering breath. It was not something he did well. He was out of practice.

But it was not what lay behind him that stole his breath; it was what lay ahead. Just beyond that threshold rose the Grande Foyer, enticing in its shifting veils of shadow and gaslight. The chantry thundered like a Victorian gasworks — the ring of hammering upon copper pipes, the roaring jets of blue flame. Silent figures slipped between the staccato bursts of fire and shadow. They went with heads bowed, arms crossed and hands concealed within long, draping sleeves.

As Emmett watched, enrapt, one of the cowled figures crossed noiselessly to a curious bank of pipes along one wall. Each of the pipes terminated in a cap of polished brass from which dangled a paper tag upon a delicate chain. The scurrying figure produced a neat scroll from one sleeve. He selected a worn leather cylinder from a recessed cubbyhole in the shadow of the array of pipes and, fumbling it open, deposited his burden. He spent some time squinting at the dangling paper tags before he found the correct one. With some effort, he prised open the brass cap and rammed the cylinder home. It whooshed upward into darkness, disappearing into the complex web of pneumatic tubes near the ceiling.

To Emmett the entire Grande Foyer seemed some elaborate clockwork toy—each gleaming brass fitting, each precisely timed jet of flame, each calculated motion of the fascinating little figurines going about their mysterious tasks. Perfect.

It was only with great effort that he wrested his gaze away. It was so easy to lose oneself here, amidst the shifting veils of desire and secrets that concealed the entry to the Tremere chantry. Emmett wanted to peel away those enticing veils, one by one, laying bare the forbidden, the sweet, supple secrets of this house. He trembled with the intensity of that desire. He was only dimly aware of the figure of the gatekeeper before him or of the uncomfortable silence that had fallen heavily between them.

"I'm here to see Sturbridge, Aisling Sturbridge," Emmett rasped out, trying to recover his composure. "She knows me." If breathing had become an unfamiliar chore for him; speaking was an effort of will. His oversized teeth scissored wetly, a sound like knives sharpening.

Talbott, the Brother Porter, stood his ground. He ran one hand through his sparse silver hair. *Once golden,* he thought absently. *Poor wages indeed for a lifetime of service to this house.* During his forty-year tenure, Talbott had ushered more than his fair share of supplicants, ambassadors, neophytes, visiting dignitaries, and the occasional stray pup through the Great Portal and into the domain of the warlocks. It had been many decades since he had shrunk back from such monstrosities as now stood before him—or, for that matter, from the often nightmarish changes they each wrought upon the Grande Foyer with their unguarded expectations and desires.

"Yes, I remember your previous visit quite well." Talbott's face was unreadable in the flickering play of light and shadow. "You had a large bundle of papers and photographs for the regent to see. But she is in the midst of some delicate researches at present and cannot be disturbed. I am sure you understand."

Emmett, taken aback at this resistance from an unexpected quarter, muttered to himself. He began pacing and then cut off abruptly. "I will wait then."

Talbott shook his head sadly. "You are, of course, welcome to wait if you would like. But between the two of us, these experiments are seldom wrapped up in less than a fortnight. It might be better if…"

Emmett was not to be put off. "I have an urgent message from Calebros. *Prince* Calebros."

If this invocation had any effect upon the gatekeeper, he gave no outward sign of this fact. "You may leave it with me, then."

"I will deliver it to Sturbridge," Emmett insisted. "The prince is awaiting her reply."

"Of course," Talbott soothed. "You may wait within. I will take your message to her." He stuck out one hand.

Emmett reluctantly handed over a plain white envelope, smudged with greasy fingerprints. Talbott was mouthing formal niceties, but Emmett barely heard him. "I am prepared to wait as long as necessary," he called absently over one shoulder. He had already turned away, his attention lost among the shifting layers of shadow and gaslight.

"I am sure you are," Talbott said. Unnoticed, he withdrew.

Chapter 6
A Gathering of Crows

Antigone sat in rigid silence throughout the remainder of the Conventicle, her hands balled into tight fists in her lap. The Rite of Drawing Down the Dragon had been her consuming focus for the past week. It was her sole reason for being here. Everything else that would happen from here on in would be mundane for her, an afternote. But she had to stay and see this whole misbegotten business through to its conclusion.

Someone needed to remain behind and take responsibility, bear the consequences. Even if all but one of her fellow conspirators remained blissfully unaware of the fact, Antigone knew—the rite had gone terribly wrong.

The next half-hour was excruciating. She endured the almost clerical litany—the list of safehouses that were no longer safe. The roster of contacts that had, since the last gathering, fallen out of contact. An entirely new set of passwords and code phrases to be committed to memory.

Antigone found her thoughts kept returning to the Wyrm-chosen, the one among their circle who had drawn the dragon. There was heat there, resentment, but she slammed the lid down on it and let it roil. *Wyrm-ridden*, she thought bitterly and smiled. It was not a pleasant sort of smile. *As in, after he screwed up my ritual, I wouldn't be caught dead in his worm-ridden carcass.*

The Bonespeaker's words had long ago ceased to register upon her thoughts. His voice droned on like a monastic chant.

Antigone thought she could detect a subtle, ominous note to it. It reminded her of storm clouds gathering.

As the litany of minutiae piled higher and higher, she found herself absently wondered how *he* would know. The Chosen was always sent away before the rest of the Conventicle, ostensibly to keep anyone from interfering with his appointed task, inadvertently or otherwise. But how, she wondered, would he know the latest signals and ciphers? How would he know to avoid the compromised dead drops? How would he...

He wouldn't, she realized with sudden clarity. That was the point. The Dragon Rite was only invoked for the most dangerous of missions. The ones that garnered the lion's share of the glory—and of the accompanying risks as well. If the Chosen were captured in the course of his mission, it would not do for him to be carrying around all the latest passwords and meeting sites in his head. Information could be extracted: that was a central tenet among the faithful—those who lived and died according to the whim of the fickle gods of knowledge and secrets.

There was a more sinister possibility of course, but Antigone was not ready to consider that at the moment: the possibility that the Chosen was never really expected to return from his assigned task at all. She recalled the feeling of solemnity when the entire circle of conspirators rose as one to honor their departing colleague. Like pall bearers stepping back from a casket.

It was the name that brought her out of her reverie. *Johanus.* Antigone's head came up sharply before she could mask her reaction. She sat very still, hoping no one had noticed her sudden interest. With a start, Antigone realized that the Litany had drawn to its conclusion some minutes before and that the Gathering of Crows was already well underway.

The Bonespeaker had resumed his seat, ceding the floor. Somewhere to her left, one of the conspirators had risen haltingly to his feet and was already addressing the assembly.

"It's like Ellis Island all over again," complained a thick Bronx accent. "I'm telling you, if he's allowed to keep at it, he's going to have every one of those damned refugees reporting directly to him. I've never seen anything like it. It's like he's trying to earmark them, sort them all out, enlist them! He's telling them where they can live, where they can feed, what they can and can't do. He's assigning them domains, for Christsakes! It's insane. I'd like to know where he gets off thinking he's got the right—or the clout—to carve up the city like that. I don't know who this guy is, or who he thinks he is, but somebody's got to shut him down cold."

He fumbled in a sack at his side and extracted a small, inert bundle. This he cast disdainfully into the center of the circle of conspirators. It landed with a thud and lay still. Antigone did not have to look to see what it was. A bundle of black feathers. The broken body of a crow, its neck neatly wrung. A silent accusation cast into their midst.

"I don't know who he is, but I can hazard a guess who he's working for." There was bitterness in the new voice. This speaker made no move to rise, but shifted uncomfortably in his seat. "This Johanus, he's a Tremere. And there's not a single one among that lot that's got the balls to stick his neck out without being damned sure he's got his ducks in a row. No, if this Johanus is trying to drum up support among the refugees, you can bet the Tremere are behind it and that they have a damned good reason for stirring things up."

"Even if he were some kind of lone wolf," a third voice interrupted. "We can't afford for a Tremere—any Tremere—to have that kind of say over what goes on in this city." He spat, mumbling something about warlocks.

"All right, agreed. It would be stupid to funnel any more power into the hands of the damned Tremere Pyramid. But if he's really doing what you say—handing out domains and havens and feeding grounds—he's stepping all over the prince's toes and doing it intentionally. That's going to cost the prince some face and weaken his position no matter how you look at it. And that's good for business."

"You want to trade a Nossie figurehead for a Tremere dictator? You've got to be off your freaking..."

"I remember this guy, Johanus, from the Liberation. Some big shot from the Chantry. Fiery red hair and beard. Always looked a little out of place, like some kind of Viking wading right through the thick of a firefight. And did he ever draw some fire. Not that I minded—"

"Gentlemen," the Bonespeaker gently interrupted. "This Johanus is obviously a warlock of some consequence and one who is not unaccustomed to the rigors of the battlefield. What action are you advocating here? The assassination of such a one is a weighty matter and perhaps one best laid directly before the dragon."

There were some murmurs of assent around the circle. Antigone knew her best course of action here was just to keep her mouth shut. But despite the risk of arousing suspicions or even possible exposure, she had to say something. To nip this particular line of speculation in the bud. Before the matter was laid before the dragon and some other damned fool drew the wrong bone and found himself committed to a suicide mission.

"I've fought beside him," She raised her voice to be sure that she was heard above the mutterings. "In the Liberation. I've seen the bastard walk right through a rain of bullets. I've seen him call down fire upon his enemies. I've seen him kill with a word. You're not going to stop somebody like that with an assassin's bullet."

At her words, the argument erupted again. In the midst of the clamor, a figure to her right strode to the center of the ring and, ignoring the commotion, took up the small, broken bird, holding it high for all to see. The room gradually quieted.

"We don't have to kill him to stop him."

Antigone was shocked at the sound of another female voice. She found herself squinting into the darkness to try to make out some hint of the other's features.

The woman in the center of the ring continued. "We can divert the flow of refugees and immigrants. They are already fearful, uncertain, fleeing from the worst excesses of the Sabbat. We can use that, feed their fear and uncertainty. When we're done, they won't dare show themselves, to him or anyone else claiming to be in authority." The broken body of the crow still dangling from one fist, she resumed her seat.

"The Redress has been taken up," the Bonespeaker quickly stepped in to restore some semblance of order. "Are there any other challenges?"

It went on this way for some time, but Antigone now had something else to worry about. She would have to get word to Johanus at the earliest opportunity. She did not know precisely what her fellow conspirator was planning, but she knew it boded ill for Johanus and his project.

Two further challenges were offered and accepted. Antigone was barely aware of them. After precisely thirty minutes, the Bonespeaker commenced the Casting Away of Stones. He circled slowly behind the ring of conspirators, three times, anticlockwise. Then he tapped one seated figure, apparently at random. Without a parting word, the figure rose and left the room. The selection was repeated at precise five-minute intervals.

There were only four of them remaining when the Bonespeaker stopped behind Antigone's chair. He laid a hand gently on her shoulder. She made no move to get up. After a moment's uncertainty, he squeezed her shoulder once and moved on, dismissing the other two conspirators in turn.

Only when the door had shut behind the last of them, did the Bonespeaker break the silence. "You are disappointed. That is understandable." He crossed to the door, secured it, and then flipped on the light switch.

Antigone sat hunched forward in the chair, elbows on thighs. She toyed idly with a small ivory tile. Turning it over and over again with one hand. Weaving it through her fingers. "Disappointed? Well, that's one way of putting it. 'Pissed off' might be another. Weeks of effort, wasted."

"Not wasted, surely. The mission will still go forward. We will knock one of the prince's crutches out from beneath him. This much I have seen."

She turned toward him as he drew closer, met his eyes. He still wore the ceremonial regalia, the cowled robe tied with the coarse rope belt. The sculpted mask was daubed a chalky white. It resembled nothing more than the skull of some predatory bird. Antigone shivered. No matter how many times she saw it, something about that mask always unsettled her. It was stupid, she knew. It was nothing more than a ceremonial tool, a construct of bark and paint and ox blood. But that didn't make it any better. There was a power to the mask, a potency. Its silent cry seemed to set up a ringing in her head, a shrill note that vibrated directly along the bones of her skull without ever traversing the intermediary of the ear.

She dropped her gaze before the expressionless avian scrutiny, her thoughts already far away. She remembered walking through the woods with her father. She could not have been more than three years old. She had broken away from him, laughing, only to stumble across, as if by chance, the small broken body of a bird.

She could vividly recall the look on Father's face when he emerged from the undergrowth to see her standing there (so very quietly), the fetid corpse clutched in one tiny white fist. There was no hint of disgust, no flicker of alarm in his face. He made no move to snatch it away from her or to get her to drop the decaying bundle of feathers. In his face she saw only a resigned sadness. The slow, patient knowing of a mountain, surrendering a well-loved icy stream to its long and solitary journey. A leave-taking.

It was all as inevitable as water flowing downhill. He took a deep breath to fortify himself for what must come next.

She held the tiny broken bundle of feathers out to him at arm's length. *"Why not fly?"* she demanded. *"Fix."*

Antigone flipped the cold ivory tile with her thumb, sending it spinning ceilingward. It was an ungainly flight. She watched it tumble end over end, the blue dragon winking at her. Once, twice, thrice…

"That was my mission. We had a deal," she said.

The tile clattered at his feet. He made no motion to catch it or pick it up. "I agree with you entirely. But things did not work out quite according to plan. Someone seems to have taken matters into his own hands. First we need to accept that and then we need to deal with the consequences."

"You can deal with the damned consequences. That was my mission. I came up with it, I planned it—I even wrote the briefing. This is all just part and parcel of the whole damned old-boys' network, isn't it? You just can't stand to think that a woman could carry off something of this importance. Well, I'm just about fed up with it. All of it. You don't think I can handle a high-profile hit? Mister, I've been in the intelligence racket since the War—the Great One. And I was good at it even back then. You don't think it's easy for a girl to break into this little perpetual gentleman's club, do you? If you knew the half of what I had to go through…"

"No one is doubting your credentials, my dear. You have nothing to prove here—"

"And if you call me 'my dear' again, I'll bust you right in the...beak." She glowered at him, holding his gaze through the slits in the stark bone mask, daring him to say anything further.

Wisely, he did not so much as crack a smile. "What would you prefer I call you?" he asked.

She considered. "You can call me Mrs. Baines."

"Missus?" he asked pointedly. "You are married? You will forgive me. It is only that you seem so young."

Antigone seethed. "So now I am too young as well as too female? Is that it? I'm out of here."

She rose but he was before her, making calming motions. "Please. Sit down. That is not what I meant at all. You know I have the utmost confidence in you, in your abilities. Otherwise I would never have agreed to your taking on this mission in the first place. You will recall that it was I who entrusted the dragon into your keeping." He scuffed the tile with his foot.

She stopped but did not return to her seat. "But you 'accidentally' put another dragon into the bag for somebody else to draw out? That's really weak."

"No, of course not. What makes you think—ah, now I see why you are so angry. Here, wait one moment." He crossed to his chair and took up the small burlap sack. Returning, he tossed the bag to her.

"Go ahead. Examine it for yourself," he said. "They are all there. Twelve winds, not a single dragon in the bunch. Go ahead, count them."

Antigone opened the sack and drew out the ivories. She examined each one in turn. "Twelve winds," she admitted reluctantly. "Then how did he..." she broke off.

"He lied," the Bonespeaker said. "I do not know his reasons. By rights, the mission was yours. We had a deal. I had given you my word. I had given you the dragon token. It only remained for the rite to progress one more place around the circle and you would have produced the tile and claimed the mission for yourself."

"Only somebody interfered with the rite," she said. "Who was it?"

"It would be a violation of trust if I were to tell you that," he said.

"Damn it, it was my rite, my mission. You think I'm just going to let something like this slide?"

"Of course not. I do not expect you to let such an affront go unpunished. But we will do things the proper way. Even assuming that I knew the identity of this man, I still could not betray it to you. It would compromise the integrity of the Conventicle."

"I'm going to track him down. You know that, right? I have...means at my disposal." The threat had little enough substance behind it, but she doubted if the Bonespeaker could know precisely what she was or was not capable of. "I will find him either way, but I would like to think that we are still on the same side. That you did not purposefully withhold information that might have been of use to me."

"Everything is so black and white with you," he said. "Helping or hindering. Friend or foe. Did I say I would not assist you? I said only that I could not reveal the man's identity. It would be a breach of trust. But I can tell you this: If he survives the mission, he will need some way to get back in touch with us."

"Because he does not know any of the new passwords and meeting places," she said. "The wyrm-chosen always leaves before the Litany."

"You are very observant, my de...Mrs. Baines," he caught himself. "He will return to the last place of contact. You will be waiting for him."

"Here," she said. "Tomorrow night?"

"Perhaps. If there are complications, it may take him longer to emerge again. But, yes, he must return here if he is to find us again."

"Then I'll wait. Thanks, you have been most…"

"Yes, it is nothing, Mrs. Baines. Good night. And good hunting."

Chapter 7
Sub Specie Aeternitatis

Calebros leaned his elbows upon the parapet, gazing down at the city spread out beneath him. The observation deck of the Empire State building was deserted, closed for the night. A cool breeze rustled across the taut parchment of his face. He smiled contentedly, a ghastly crack splitting the deathmask. This was one of the few open, aboveground places where he felt safe. He stubbornly ignored all evidence to the contrary—the dizzying height, the police helicopter that banked a bit too close, the rumble of the old elevator clawing its way up from the eighty-sixth floor.

He thought he had locked down the elevator manually after his arrival. Emmett had shown him how to do it, once. *He* would know. Absently, Calebros marked the elevator's progress, but his eyes never left the city. *My city*, he thought, *Lord help them.*

Some skeptical part of his mind kept reminding him that it was not the city that he was seeing at all—not the real city. The real city was the one that concealed itself behind this brilliant neon veil. From the coquettish wink of the marquees he could only deduce the grand old ladies of Broadway—the historic theatres past their prime but still dolling themselves up in layer upon layer of phosphorescent makeup. From the screaming logos blazing forth from Times Square he could derive the presence of the babbling media giants, blaring inanities into the night sky. Television and radio waves ricocheted aimlessly between distant stars. *Sub specie aeternitatis.*

Far below, minute antennae-like headlights tested the walls of the labyrinth, scurrying through the invisible grid of right-angle turnings and one-way streets that could only be inferred from the curious darting lights themselves. The logic of the city was circular. It asserted nothing, proved nothing.

If there was any substance there at all, behind the gauzy layers of shimmering light, it had to be approached stealthily and caught unawares. Behind him, the elevator doors sighed open. The chime that traditionally announced the elevator's arrival was conspicuously absent. It was possible that it had gone out of order since Calebros's own ascent, he mused. But it seemed far more likely that it had been disabled. Calebros did not turn toward the opening doors, but instead purposefully set his back to them and crossed to the nearest chrome viewing device. He withdrew a rotting burlap sack from inside one sleeve and fumbled around in it for an appropriate coin.

The approaching footfalls were nearly imperceptible. The rasping voice, when it came, sounded soft and directly behind him. "It's the one with the eagle on one side and the bald guy on the other. That's George Washington. It's big, silver, and has a serrated edge. Why didn't you lock down the elevator like I showed you?"

"Thank you, Emmett," Calebros replied somewhat testily. "I think I know what a quarter is. Damned new-fangled coinage..." Calebros interposed the breadth of his back between Emmett and the coin slot.

"I said the bald guy. That's Kennedy; he's got hair. And it's clearly not going to fit in that little slot. Here, let me."

Calebros hunched further over the purse, shielding it from Emmett's groping hand. Emmett struggled only a moment longer before abandoning the effort as a lost cause. "Forget it. Look, *this* is a quarter." He extracted a coin from his pocket, brandishing it at Calebros. Reaching past the prince, he inserted it into the slot. There was a rattling noise and then a sharp clack.

"You look through these two little holes here..." Emmett began, but broke off under the withering look of his superior.

Calebros pivoted the viewer, searching the press of buildings for the shadowy true forms behind the concealing blaze of lights. "Infernal contraption..." he muttered. He turned his attention to the lights peeking from the hotel-room windows just down the block. "Can't see a damned thing through this." He clouted the viewer resoundingly in frustration. The metal support, as thick around as a strong man's arm, bent noticeably.

"Easy! You'll throw it out of alignment." Emmett shouldered past him and tried, in vain, to straighten it back up.

"Alignment?!" Calebros snorted. "I just told you the foul thing is malfunctioning. Is a good, old-fashioned spyglass too much to ask for? You'd think that when they spring something like this on you—when they stick you with rebuilding the last Camarilla stronghold on the whole Eastern Seaboard—that they could at least throw in a damned spyglass. Is that too much to ask?"

Emmett pointedly ignored his prince's tirade. He took a ring of at least fifty keys from the pocket of his oil-stained coat. Methodically he worked his way through the tangle of keys until he found the right one. Stretching around to the back of the viewer, he inserted the key and turned. The back panel, hinged at the bottom, opened to reveal a delicate array of electronics. Emmett reached into the tangle of exposed innards and flipped a switch. He was rewarded with three blinking red lights and a mechanical whirring as the antenna struggled to establish the satellite uplink.

"Come on..." he coaxed. One by one, the indicator lights went green. "Yes!"

He turned to Calebros in undisguised triumph, but immediately deflated upon seeing the pained expression on his superior's face. It was a look one might give a cat who had just proudly deposited a dead bird at your feet. "I take it that means that you've fixed the blasted thing." Calebros said.

Emmett grunted and gestured toward the viewer. As if expecting to receive an electric shock, Calebros tentatively took the handles and leaned into the eyeholes. "Well, that's a little better," he admitted grudgingly. The hotel-room window, which had previously appeared a vague rectangle of light, now surrendered its secrets. On the little table near the bed, he could clearly pick out the logo of the hotel stationery as well as the name and phone number hastily scrawled there. Adam Graves. A local number. Calebros made a mental note.

Calebros swept the viewer away from the bustle of the theatre district and toward Morningside Heights and the secluded campus of Barnard College. He zoomed in on the silent Millbank Hall. The campus administrative building had the ambiguous distinction of being the most public approach to the subterranean Chantry of Five Boroughs—the domain of the warlocks.

"You have not told me how Regent Sturbridge reacted to our invitation tonight, Emmett?"

Emmett shifted uncomfortably, a fact which was not lost on his superior, despite the fact that he never glanced up from the viewer. "Never saw her. That watchdog of hers, Talbott, he said she was in the middle of some hocus pocus and couldn't be disturbed."

At this Calebros did turn upon him, but Emmett forestalled the expected rebuke with a raised hand. "I insisted, of course, but it was no good. In the end I got him to take her your note at least. Here's her reply." He handed over an envelope that bore the distinct appearance of old vellum. The front of the envelope was bare of all writing. On the back, it bore only a single letter, an illuminated 'C' positioned directly across the flap of the envelope like a seal.

Calebros sliced along the top seam with one blackened fingernail, cautiously avoiding all contact with the seal. He unfolded and quickly scanned the epistle within. He seemed about to say something, then stopped himself and reread the letter. This time much more slowly.

"Have you seen the contents of this letter?" Calebros's voice was raised not so much in anger as in disbelief.

"Are you insane? No offense. You really think I'm stupid enough to poke my nose into anything that comes out of a Tremere chantry? I don't know if I would have opened that damned letter if it were addressed to *me*."

Calebros treated his broodmate to his most patient look, the one he usually reserved for idiots and children. Emmett fidgeted under the withering gaze. "But I don't really have to read the note, do I? I got the gist of it clear enough. Just from watching that gatekeeper, Talbott. She ain't coming, is she?"

"Look at this." Calebros extended the letter and, when Emmett hesitated, shook it at him. He seemed eager to be rid of it. Emmett took the sheet and scanned the brief but polite refusal:

> *To:Calebros, Prince*
> *From:Sturbridge, Regentia, C5B*
>
> *Thank you for your generous invitation. I am desolated that I shall be unable to attend. I am, at present, engaged in the rather delicate task of smoking out the remnant of the Koldun infestation. I am sure you will understand that this is a responsibility that can neither be lightly set aside nor entrusted to less experienced hands.*

> *It is unlikely that I shall be able to break away*
> *before another fortnight has passed. I shall look*
> *forward to meeting with you upon my return to*
> *discuss the administrative details you mentioned*
> *in your note.*

> *Fide et Vigilante,*

> *—A.S.*

"Yep. Looks like she ain't coming. So now what?" Emmett tried to hand the letter back, but the prince ignored him.

"Do you notice anything unusual about that note?"

Emmett frowned and skimmed the page again. "Yeah, more Kolduns. Nice of her to mention it. Would have been even nicer to have known about it yesterday before we green-lighted that sweep down by the Battery. I've still got two patrols that haven't checked back in yet. We've got sniffers out there, going back over those patrol routes, but it's been over twenty-four hours. I'm not real optimistic at this point."

Calebros's hands wrung the railing more tightly, drawing a metallic squeal of protest. More unwelcome news. His immediate instinct was to pounce, to grill his subordinate for details, to demand why he hadn't been informed earlier. It took an effort of will to fight down this urge. Deliberately, he drew breath and held it until he had calmed. He knew all that could be done was already being done.

"Do you know," he mused aloud, "that in the olden days we had this quaint custom of summarily executing the bearers of such tidings? Perhaps I'm merely being nostalgic, but these nights I find myself sorely tempted to reinstate this charming tradition."

"Suit yourself." Emmett shrugged. "But it seems to me that you're going to wind up with more dead messengers than good news to show for your trouble."

Calebros smiled his deathmask smile. "I have nothing against dead messengers. Of late, I find myself employing them almost to the exclusion of all others. No, the problem isn't that their bodies are dead, it's that their wits have decayed. Look at that letter again. Do you notice anything out of the ordinary about the note itself? I don't mean its contents."

Emmett turned first the letter and then the envelope over carefully, but failed to discover anything out of the ordinary. "Like what?"

"Like the handwriting for starters. It's not Sturbridge's."

"What do you mean, it's not hers?" Emmett demanded. "Of course it's hers. Who else's could it be? Why would anybody be so stupid as to…" He let the question trail off.

"To forge this note? Yes, why indeed? There are too many unknowns here." Calebros mused for a time, his fingers drumming out a slow, hypnotic rhythm atop the chrome viewer. "But I think we might narrow the field of possibilities a bit. To my mind, the crux of the puzzle boils down to two significant scenarios. All other answers fall under the umbrella of one of these two solutions."

"You mean either someone is screwing with us, or this is just some lame Tremere stab at a practical joke."

Calebros scowled at him. "You disappoint me, Emmett. It is a constant source of amazement to me how you can, at a glance, trace every twisting in this rat's nest of wires, but at the same time utterly fail to extricate yourself from the simplest of logical knots. Your choices do not comprise the totality. There are a wealth of other possibilities that do not fall beneath either of your two umbrellas. Shall I give you an example?"

"Name three," Emmett challenged, a bit belligerently.

"All right. First of all, there are a few perfectly innocent explanations for why Sturbridge's handwriting might not appear on this note. Possibility the first: Sturbridge routinely employs an intermediary to handle all correspondences. A personal secretary would certainly be in keeping with her station and the custom of her mortal days. She is the product of a more genteel age, the turn of the century if I recall correctly. The *last* century," he clarified.

"Yeah, but no personal secretary is going to take it upon himself to decline a formal invitation from the prince," Emmett retorted. "He's still going to consult with Sturbridge."

"Unless he cannot," Calebros said. "Possibility the second: the situation is exactly as presented in this note. Sturbridge is presently steeped to the elbows in the spilling blood of some thaumaturgic rite. Disturbing her would undo weeks of effort. The chantry's second-in-command has been instructed and authorized to act *in loco regentiae* for the ritual's duration."

Smiling, Emmett pounced. "But you didn't pick this explanation as your first choice, did you? You don't buy it. You're just playing devil's advocate. You *do* think somebody's screwing with us."

"You may call me a skeptic, but I do not think absolute honesty is the most probable solution here," Calebros grudgingly agreed. "I must admit the scenario that weighs most heavily upon my thoughts is more sinister. Possibility the third: consider for a moment that Regent Sturbridge may very well be dead."

"Dead?! You think she's dead? That's going to throw a bit of a wrench into your dinner plans."

Calebros ignored his outburst. "Her subordinates would not like this fact to become known, of course, before a replacement can be selected. Their position would be suddenly…precarious."

"You said it. Anyone with an axe to grind against the Tremere might take it as an ideal opportunity for a little revenge. You really think she's dead?"

Calebros rubbed at he eyes. He looked weary. "I said that I feared that she may be. We haven't heard anything from her since the confirmation that the Tremere had completed their end of the bargain in that nasty business with Leopold and the Eye. Make a note to check the handwriting on that correspondence as well, Emmett. It is entirely possible that she might have fallen in that battle. The clash of arcane energies did manage to take out the better part of a city block of prime Manhattan real estate. Sturbridge, however, is one tough lady. It might take more than that put her out of commission."

Emmett nodded his acknowledgement, scribbling a few cryptic symbols in a pudgy grade-school pocket notebook. Calebros continued dictating: "I need the chantry's main entrance, Millbank Hall, watched around the clock. That and any other points of egress we've isolated. I just want a fly on the wall. Nobody makes any unscheduled contact with the Tremere, period. Nothing short of an emergency medical intervention, you understand?"

Emmett flipped the notebook closed. "No problem. Seems to me I got the easy part. Meanwhile, you get stuck with trying to hold the whole damned city together single-handedly. You going to be able to pull this one off? If we can't count on any support from the Tremere, I mean."

Calebros did not answer right away. "We've got to use the Tremere absence to our advantage. Leak the word that we've got the goods on Sturbridge and that she doesn't dare even poke her head up out of that hole of hers. Or tell them that I've promised to hand over the entire city to her—lock, stock, and barrel—when my term here is done. No, better still. Let both rumors circulate a bit. If the Tremere are hurt, we've got to buy them some time to regroup. If the other factions think

Sturbridge's hands are tied, they will make sympathetic overtures. At least initially."

Emmett looked doubtful, but the prince pressed on. "And if the Tremere are, as you so colorfully put it, 'screwing with us,' we need to supply everyone else with some pretty strong reasons to move against the warlocks before the year is out. Setting Sturbridge up as the heir apparent should do the trick."

"You know, you were never this mean before they made you prince," Emmett said.

"I was; I just wasn't as forthcoming about it. I fear I'm losing my subtlety. These new responsibilities do nothing but draw one out into the open."

Emmett waved away the prince's concern. "That's only so their snipers can get a better shot at you."

Instinctively Calebros found his eyes scanning the nearby rooftops for the telltale hint of moonlight on gunmetal. "Let's go down, the night is getting cool." Reluctantly, he turned his back upon the veiled cityscape.

Emmett chuckled, a low, grating sound like slates being ground together, and pulled open the door leading back into the glass-walled visitor's center. A flicker of annoyance crossed his features. "Damn it. I know I locked down that…"

The light above the elevator doors blinked to life accompanied, not by the traditional musical chime (which had been disabled), but by the guttering roar of a fireball erupting from the closed confines of the elevator car. The explosion rocked the entire structure. The floor pitched like the deck of a storm-tossed ship. The glass walls shattered outward into the night.

Emmett had only a moment's warning—time enough to instinctively lose his grip on the doorpull and pitch himself face down upon the concrete. The wave of flying shards broke over him. A fraction of a second later, he felt the whoosh of the billowing flames. They raced, laughing, the length of his prone form. Then the concerns of the flesh receded a pace, rendered somehow irrelevant by the all-consuming immediacy of his own screams, the terror and the gnashing of the Beast.

Calebros was not so lucky. The blossoming flower of fire and glass caught him head on. Instantly it tattered his clothing, peppering his moldering flesh with raw red weals as it plucked him effortlessly up and over the parapet.

Chapter 8
Dreams of the Father

Helena spent yet another fitful day's rest in the regent's sanctum. At least her repose was untroubled by nightmares of the Children Down the Well. She had not been visited by *les tremeres* since the night they had found Sturbridge's body in the crypts. *The same night this damnable bleeding started*, she thought.

Tonight, as soon as she awoke, Helena realized that all was not well. She rose from the nest she had smoothed out for herself in Sturbridge's tumbledown throne of books, stretching and scanning the room. She had worked the worst of the kinks out of her neck and back before she realized what was wrong.

The first thing was the hum from the monitor on the bedside table. It had not been turned on when she had laid the staked regent back into her bed. Helena was sure of it.

The second thing that was wrong was that one section of the bedcurtains had been torn entirely from the cast-iron canopy and lay crumpled in a ball on the floor. Last night, they had been torn loose, but still dangled from their customary perch.

With growing anxiety, Helena confirmed the third thing that was amiss: Sturbridge was gone.

The bedsheets were puddled with stagnant water, dotted with the odd strand of matted hair, the ragged scrap of bluish flesh, the stub of a single whitened fingernail. In the precise center of the bed lay the wooden stake. Helena extended her hand slowly and took it up. The wood was stained dark, saturated with stagnant water. It squelched in her hand. Soft, pulpy, the fibrous threads unraveled in her grasp. As if the stake had been many years beneath the waters.

Propped upright on the pillow, well above the high-water mark, was a single neat piece of stationery. It was folded in half and stood erect like a pyramid. Helena wiped the wood pulp from her hand upon the bedcurtains and turned over the note.

> *Helena,*
>
> *Perhaps I phrased that poorly. All is well. As well as can be expected. Perhaps better than can be explained.*
>
> *Eva is utterly dead and beyond harm. It seems the rest of us may not have been as fortunate. I think it will be quite some time before we can fully grasp, much less begin to heal, the injury she has inflicted upon us. Even as you slumber, I can feel your hurt. I can smell your blood upon you and I know what it is that you suffer. This affliction that is upon me, it has much the same source.*
>
> *You were much closer to the truth than I was ready to admit when you insisted that I had eaten our dead. I know that sounds monstrous but there is no other way that I can say it or understand it at present. Not physically eaten them, of course. That would be merely ghoulish. But I have devoured them—the Children, the nightmares, les tremeres. Swallowed them utterly.*

I am watching you now, as you slumber. Do you see them still, I wonder? The Children, the reproachful, self-incriminating dreams of the Father. Or do they belong to me and me alone now? One thing is certain: Eva wanted to be free of the nightmare. In this she succeeded beyond her wildest expectations. Within the walls of this chantry, she may be condemned as a murderer, but beyond? It may be that to those who will come after us, she will be hailed as the hero, if not the redeemer, of our line.

I must go. Too much has been left undone too long. Know that I forgive you. But do not be here when I return.

—A.S.

P.S. The security clearance hierarchy is a wreck. Casualties. Please update.

Helena crushed the note in her fist. *Sturbridge had lost it.* There was no other explanation. She caught herself in the middle of angrily casting away the wad of paper and reconsidered. When trouble came of this—and there was little doubt at this point that trouble would come of this—she might need some hard evidence of Sturbridge's present mindset. It might help at least to deflect some measure of the doom that was likely to be, even now, descending upon them.

One thing was certain. Sturbridge could not be allowed to remain at large in her current condition. Helena would have to come up with some more effectual way of subduing her until the special ops from Vienna arrived.

Smoothing the wrinkles from the note as best she could, she turned and stalked from the sanctum.

Chapter 9
The Underlined Ones are Dead

The gymnasium had the air of a war room about it. There were nine distinct stations, each made up of a pair of folding banquet tables that had been hastily commandeered and shoved together. Each station boasted a knot of increasingly irate Kindred and a huge aerial map attached to the double tabletop with masking tape. The maps were already quite worn from extensive handling, and covered with cryptic markings in bright magic marker. Hanging pasteboard signs over the nine stations read: *Brooklyn, Queens, Bronx, Staten Island, Manhattan, North Jersey, Upstate, Connecticut* and *Undercity*, respectively.

Johanus stood in the midst of the maelstrom, Kindred refugees and immigrants streaming around him. He barely saw their faces anymore. He was bent with weariness. His lips moved mechanically, as if repeating a familiar mantra for comfort. The angry responses that punctuated his pronouncements were utterly lost upon him.

"No, there is no sign-up table for eastern Pennsylvania," he recited woodenly.

[haughty question]

"Because there are no feeding grounds available there."

[objection, counter-proposition]

"*Especially* not in the direction of Philadelphia."

[indignant outburst]

"Yes, but unfortunately the City of Brotherly Love has been a Sabbat stronghold for some time now. Try something in the Bronx. There are still some available sectors there."

Johanus turned toward the next supplicant in the mob that blocked his path to the exit. "Yes, you are correct. You cannot claim Central Park as your personal domain. That is why it is marked in red."

[question embedded in anatomically unlikely suggestion]

"Or perhaps it is because it is infested with Lupines."

[angry pause. Further impolite inquiry from another direction]

"I believe you are thinking of the Plaza Hotel. The Crown Plaza is the one that was demolished last month."

[growing exasperation]

"Definitely not. You will notice that the Plaza Hotel abuts the Park. Someone at the Manhattan station can point out the four- and five-star hotels for you, if that is your criteria for selecting a haven. If you will excuse me…"

It took him no less than half an hour to fight his way through the press of cold bodies to the far wall. He banged through the swinging doors and into the comparative silence of the empty hallway beyond. The high school was deserted for the evening. Both the late-night custodian and security guard had been replaced with Johanus's own agents. He made his way to a modest wooden door labeled *Boiler Room: Maintenance Staff Only*. Unlocking it, he descended the darkened stair into the vast basement.

He could barely pick out the form of Umberto seated near the far wall. His back was to the stairway as he hunched over a computer keyboard. The Nosferatu was a mere silhouette against the three huge forty-two-inch computer monitors blazing before him. They enclosed him in a three-walled shield, half a hexagon.

"With you in just a sec," Umberto called over his shoulder, in answer to the footfalls on the metal steps.

"Take your time," Johanus replied. Making his way around the imposing bulk of the old boiler, he flopped down an intimidating pile of paperwork on the already cluttered desk next to Umberto. With visible relief, Johanus sank into an overstuffed armchair that smelled strongly of mildew. He ignored it. "I'm not in any hurry to get back out there."

He closed his eyes and listened to the hypnotic tap of the keyboard, losing himself to it. Almost, it seemed, he could pick out the meaning of what Umberto was typing just from the rhythm of the keystrokes. There was a code there somewhere. Not the staccato dots and dashes of the telegraph operator. Nor even the nervous ten-key and triumphant spooling of the adding machine. No, the computer keyboard had its own rhythms, its own music.

Johanus understood the meaning of that code only too well. There was no mistaking the mood of Umberto's fugue. Nor was there any evading the conclusion to which it was drawing him. But Johanus asked anyway. He had to. Perhaps he only wanted to know that someone else grasped the danger. "What's the damage, Umberto?"

Another sharp burst of keystrokes. Umberto turned to the monitor at his right hand. The picture was divided into nine panels. A tic-tac-toe board. The panels displayed the live feed from concealed cameras above each of the stations in the gymnasium.

Umberto tapped the square showing the map of the Bronx. The image appeared in close-up on the monitor at his left hand—the minute maze of scribblings that covered its surface magnified and laid bare. "Just updating the latest changes now." He keyed in the overlay of the saved map information and sat back rubbing the bridge of his nose with both hands while he waited for the pictures to click into alignment.

"All right, now we just transfer the differences to the master. I'll put the visual up here for you. I know you only look at the pictures anyway." He smiled as the lines of blinking green characters that crowded the central monitor vanished. For an instant, Johanus caught a glimpse of something monolithic, something monstrous, flashing across the screen. It was an abstract representation of the raw datastructure—a skyscraper of screaming neon data.

Then it too was gone, consumed by the composite image that blazed forth from the screen—the entire city of New York and its environs. It was not the city as any of its nineteen million diurnal residents would see it. It was a city on the very shore of night. A city locked in perpetual pre-dawn twilight.

Umberto tapped the legend box in the corner of the map and checked the bottom line again to be sure. Then he let out a long, low whistle. "All told? One hundred twenty-seven. And that's only the ones who have registered. There've got to be at least a couple of dozen folks who've decided to buck tradition and just not bother with presenting themselves to the prince upon arrival. And *that's* not counting the ones who are just wandering around lost, or confused, or abandoned, or not knowing any better, or…"

"All right, I get the picture. What the hell are we going to do with them all?"

For the first time, Umberto turned away from the bank of monitors. Seen straight-on, his head looked soft and mushy, like a moldy apple. The entire section of skull above his right eye had fallen in under its own weight. He shrugged, a gesture which looked as if it might dislodge his lolling head altogether. But his eye was steady and shrewd as it fixed on Johanus. "I imagine we'll just wait for most of them to kill one another off."

Johanus snorted his disapproval and pushed himself from his chair. "That's not a plan, that's an admission of defeat. Calebros isn't going to be able to maintain even a semblance of control if these guys can get away with killing each other in the street. Any outbreak of violence is going to have to be answered swiftly and in kind."

"Same difference," Umberto shrugged. "Either way, it means there's a little bit more real estate to go around. Speaking of which," he ignored Johanus's rising objection and tore a scroll of paper from the printer. "Here's last night's Recycle List—it's got all the domains, havens, feeding grounds and what-have-you that were previously assigned but are now 'available' again."

Johanus snatched the proffered list. "You're telling me all these folks are dead? That they died last night?!"

Umberto's tone was matter-of-fact. "Not all of them. A bunch of them decided the digs were not to their liking. Some are back here tonight to try their luck again. Others, no doubt, have given up on the system and decided to strike out on their own. The *underlined* ones are dead."

"Oh, that's a nice touch," Johanus shot back. He began to pace. "Do we know who is responsible? Is Calebros aware of these murders?"

"He's got to know. Some of those underscores are our own guys," Umberto admitted. "We lost two patrols last night, down in the Battery."

Johanus wheeled upon him. "Two patrols? That's not some squabble over prime hunting grounds. That's armed resistance. Show me on the map."

Umberto hesitated only a moment, but it was enough. For Johanus, it was like being doused with a bucket of cold water. He was abruptly reminded that, no matter how closely they had worked together during the past week, and no matter how much they might like to pretend otherwise, he and Umberto were ultimately not playing for the same team. The Nosferatu was holding something back.

"Um, sure. Here you go. It's right down here." Umberto turned away to cover his embarrassment. He fumbled for the zoom key and tapped the map once, twice, thrice. With each tap, Johanus felt as if he were plunging headfirst toward the pavement below. As he steadied himself, Umberto attacked the keyboard. Two snaking lines, one red and one green, wound toward each other through the maze of streets.

"Both patrol routes run pretty close to the docks, right about there. This whole area was pretty thick with Sabbat packs before the Liberation. That's why we were running these sweeps in the first place. Looks like the conquering heroes must have missed a knot of them."

Johanus wondered at the note of bitterness in his companion's voice. Conquering heroes? In Umberto's mouth, the words sounded like an accusation. What beef could the Nosferatu have with Bell, Pieterzoon and the other Camarilla bigwigs that had broken the Sabbat stranglehold on New York? Sure, the assault was directly responsible for the fix they now found themselves in—trying to cope with the overwhelming press of refugees, immigrants, opportunists, prospectors, pariahs, carpetbaggers, Anarchs, pioneers, outlaws—all the usual debris that rushed in to fill a power vacuum. Everybody had a dream, or at least, a scheme.

But Johanus was no green newcomer to the city. He had endured for decades under the ever-increasing pressure of the Sabbat thumb. The Chantry of Five Boroughs had had the double-edged honor of being the final pocket of resistance in the war-torn city. But it had endured. It had become the bulwark against which the rising Sabbat tide—which had already swallowed the entirety of the East Coast—had finally broken and been thrown back.

But that victory had not been without its cost. Johanus winced away from the thought, reproaching himself for the solemn duties he had left neglected all this week. Duties to his house, his clan, his brethren, his regent, and to the novices entrusted to his personal care.

Neglected? More like *avoided*. There was no use trying to couch it in euphemisms. As if to condemn him further, his thoughts instinctively flew to his rightful place—at Sturbridge's side. He should go to her. He would go to her. Soon now. Honestly.

"Don't worry, we've got folks out looking for them. Good folks. They'll find them," Umberto soothed, misinterpreting the cause of the adept's sudden silence.

Johanus shook himself and stretched. "Yeah, I know they will." He clapped Umberto on the shoulder. "But I can't wait up for them. Not tonight. I'm about beat and I've got hours of work waiting for me back at the chantry. You can finish up here?"

"Sure thing. Go home. Get some rest. I'll even make sure nobody stakes any claims to your little piece of the action near the Park...."

That quip managed to break in upon Johanus's brooding. "Yeah, and remember I've got dibs on the private pleasure dome up in the torch of the Statue of Liberty, too. Don't even get me started on our new neighbors...."

"Deal. I thought you were getting out of here?"

"I am. But I want to see that thing one more time before I go. The one that flashed up right before the composite picture."

Umberto looked puzzled. "What, you mean this?" He toggled back to the command screen and its crowd of blinking green letters.

"No, the one right after that. Call up the composite again. There!" It flickered and was gone again instantly, replaced by the familiar aerial view of the city.

Having caught the trailing end of the thread he sought, however, Johanus was not about to let go until he had worked it loose. "Can you make it so that it does all its calculations and stuff and then just waits for about a minute before displaying the map?"

"I imagine so...." Umberto was doubtful, not seeing what the warlock was driving at. "Like this?"

The intricate datastructure flared to life and hung there before them, a delicate and radiant crystal. Johanus drew a sharp, involuntary breath, and Umberto turned a curious look upon him.

But Johanus ignored him. He had eyes only for the screen and the radiant construct unfolding there like a blossoming flower of fire and glass. Johanus found himself being drawn deeper into the elaborate, gleaming pattern. He reached out a tentative hand, straining to trace the razor-sharp lines with his fingertips, to caress them. In vain, his mind raced across the crystal's surface, striving to grasp the precise number of its facets. It was a fool's quest, a mental calculation that was unlikely to be carried off without recourse to scientific notation.

As Johanus peered deeper into the ethereal construct, however, the vision shifted and took on a more sinister aspect. He could now see that there were fine lines running throughout the crystal—a web of hairline faults which a master gemcutter might exploit to shatter the improbable jewel. As Johanus watched, enrapt, these fault lines seemed to curl up at the edges, to twist and writhe. The sigils revealed in the depths of the crystal hinted at forbidden shapes, blasphemous patterns, monstrous diagramma.

Then, just as suddenly as it had been conjured up, the spell was broken. The screen dimmed, the radiant image fading to black.

"Where did it go?" Johanus demanded. "Bring it back."

"Well, I'll be damned. *That's* what you were looking for? That's nothing but the raw data—the afterimage of all that graphic input being analyzed, interpreted and pigeonholed into the datastructures we've set up here. That and the quick bursts of calculations that render it all into the pixel city that you and I can understand and ogle over. It's nothing to get all…what's wrong?"

"And the cracks, the fractures in the jewel?"

"The jewel? That's a funny way of looking at it." Umberto considered. "I don't know. Empty data fields I imagine. Incomplete information. Could be unassigned values or null pointers or any number of things. I didn't catch more than a glimpse of it and I couldn't say much of anything definitively without getting in there and digging a little. Why are you so interested in the underlying data structures all of a sudden? You've never taken any interest in the nuts and bolts before. No offense."

"I'm interested because what I just saw didn't look like any 'datastructure' to me. It looked like a very complex and very potent hermetic sigil—some kind of glyph, or a warding. Perhaps, a seal."

The basement had fallen very silent. Umberto shifted uncomfortably. "I don't think I like where you're going with this. I've got this sick feeling you're about to tell me that there's some kind of sinister pattern to all this. Some hidden cipher to this horde of refugees—to their exact numbers, their dates of arrival, their ambitions, their grossly underinformed choices of haven and feeding grounds. You know, there's a really good reason that nobody hangs out with you guys."

"All I'm saying," Johanus said, his tone the more troubling for its total lack of emotion. "Is that we have just spent the last week unwittingly constructing an incredibly elaborate hermetic diagram, the purpose of which is, at present, hidden from me."

Umberto cursed quietly, grinding the heel of his palms into his eye sockets. "You'd better pull up a chair. I'm going in, but I'm going to need you to tell me when I'm getting too close to something that's going to burn me. You need to make any calls? It looks like it's going to be a long night."

Chapter 10
The Nolo Te Intrare

Antigone stormed into the security-control room. The chantry's autonomic defense systems were keening out an integrity failure. It had been weeks since the last real emergency, if you could call it an emergency. She called it "the day the nightmares stopped"—largely because she still had no idea what to make of the strange signs and portents.

Not that she had much opportunity to discuss it. The others, they mostly pretended that nothing out of the ordinary had happened at all. She had been unable to find anyone except Helena who was even willing to admit to the Children's existence, much less their inexplicable departure. And she hadn't seen Helena since.

That in itself was nothing unusual. With Sturbridge in critical condition and Johanus tied up in the herculean task of coordinating the relief effort for the refugees, all of the night-to-night administrative details of running the chantry would land squarely in Helena's lap. Add to that her normal security duties and that must have left the adepta with more than her hands full.

Trying to ignore the earsplitting alarms, Antigone crossed to the main exchange and keyed an aleph-level override—a code sequence which identified her as the ranking on-duty security officer. Nothing.

Almost lost beneath the banshee wail, a maddeningly calm female voice repeated, "Systems warning: Integrity failure. Location: Novice *domicilium*. Nature of failure: Dangerous degradation of spirit warding. Breach imminent." There was a crisp, almost laughing singsong to the voice—a musical lilt reminiscent of the south of Ireland.

Antigone was always taken aback by the voice. She had grown accustomed to the guttural male Germanic tones of the chantry's previous security daemon. She could vividly recall Helena's black mood when Sturbridge had first casually suggested the change. It had taken Helena the better part of a month to bind and integrate that spirit into the very crux of the chantry defensive network. But to her credit, Helena never uttered a single word of complaint about the regent's unusual request—especially in front of the newly founded team.

Sturbridge's demanding timetable—which Helena paraphrased as "yesterday if not sooner"—had forced the security chief to recruit and train an entire team where previously she had taken sole responsibility for the chantry's defenses. Yes, it had been an inhuman burden, but few would make the mistake of pegging Helena as merely human.

Antigone had to admire Helena for her composure, for her restraint, and for her grim determination to carry off seemingly impossible tasks—even when the reasons behind them were not entirely clear to her.

But Antigone also had sense enough to keep her head down and to stay out of Helena's way as much as possible during the hellish weeks that followed. The experience of trying to unbind the system's controlling spirit without destroying the entire delicate network of electronic, mechanical and arcane defenses, was not a performance she was anxious to repeat any century soon.

If there were any positive side to this travail, it was that Antigone—and the rest of the new security team—now knew the system inside and out. They had pretty much had to dismantle and rebuild the whole grid from scratch.

A less experienced operator, faced with the present wailing alarms, might have kept typing and retyping passwords when the system failed to acknowledge her code sequence. Antigone, however, knew that such efforts would be fruitless. She knew enough to be worried. A fine film of blood sweat stood out on her forehead.

"Code level necessary to override?" she barked.

"Gimel-level override required. Please summon Sturbridge, Regentia or Helena, Adepta."

"Where are they? I mean, 'Location of Sturbridge, Regentia, and Helena, Adepta?'" *Why didn't Helena answer that damned alarm? You can hear the keening all over the chantry.*

"Checking clearance. Aleph-level. Approved. Sturbridge, Regentia, is currently located in regent's sanctum. Communication node disabled. Helena, Adepta, is currently located in regent's sanctum. Communication node disabled. Helena, Adepta, is currently located in Hall of Audience. Communication node disabled. Unauthorized thaumaturgic ritual in progress. Local defensive system warning: Override status."

Antigone cursed and started from the room in the direction of the Hall of Audience. If Helena had shut down both the communications ports, that meant she had a pretty good reason not to be disturbed. To Antigone's mind, that said that Sturbridge's condition had worsened. But it didn't seem like Antigone had much option at this point except to intrude.

At the doorway, she stopped suddenly, struck by something the security daemon had said. She turned and again called "Location of Helena, Adepta?"

"Helena, Adepta, is currently located in regent's sanctum. Communication node disabled. Helena, Adepta, is currently located in Hall of Audience. Communication node disabled.

Unauthorized thaumaturgic rite in progress. Local defensive system warning: Override status."

There it was again. The first time Antigone had heard the message, she'd thought that it meant that Helena was on the move, leaving the sanctum and entering the adjoining audience hall. She would be conjuring up her defenses as she came — and thus the hasty, unauthorized thaumaturgic effect — readying herself to cope with the present crisis. But the security daemon seemed to be insisting that Helena was still in the regent's sanctum as well. The system integrity failure must be more extensive than Antigone had thought.

She hurried from the room and down the corridor, accompanied by the blaring of alarms. The corridors were unsettlingly empty. Turning a corner, she nearly collided with one of her fellow novices. There was a look of undisguised terror in his eyes, the dim afterimages of flames and of the pawings of the Beast.

He frantically pushed away from her and scrambled up the corridor, away from the novice *domicilium*. Over his shoulder he cursed and spat something about "jackals." Antigone forced herself to let him go.

She was running by the time she turned into the Hall of Daggers and Mirrors, the long, sweeping skirts of her robes billowing out behind her. She was so rattled that she stumblingly triggered no fewer than three defensive systems before reaching the portal to the audience hall. She was rewarded with a renewed wave of blaring alarms and systems warnings that she had no time to deal with right now. The sight of the portal into the Hall of Audience brought her up short.

There was a piece of parchment nailed to the great oak panels by means of a wicked, stiletto-thin blade. A shard of onyx. The parchment seemed to wriggle upon the knifepoint as if trying to work its way free. On the parchment, two words stood out boldly. The letters, rendered in blood, were dried and already flaking under the parchment's contortions.

Nolo Te Intrare.

Antigone cursed and jerked her hand back from the door as if coming within a hairsbreadth of brushing against a sleeping serpent. She looked around helplessly, searching for someone or something else to throw against the warding. She yelled for Helena, fighting down the instinctive urge to hammer upon the portal—a course of action which might well prove disastrous. She was afraid even to touch the doors at all, lest she inadvertently trigger the warding. There was no reply from within.

She quickly abandoned this unproductive line of attack. She doubted whether Helena—if she were, in fact, within—would have even heard her call when she had failed to note the blaring alarms from this side of the doorway.

The other alternative was even less pleasant. Antigone shook her head sharply and pushed the thought down and away. She was not eager to entertain the possibility that Helena had heard, but was unable to respond—lying hurt, or unconscious, or—

Squeezing her eyes shut and clenching her teeth, Antigone put one hand out to the polished copper door pull. The chill of the ice-smooth metal raced the length of her arm and washed over her like a wave of relief. So far, so good. She muttered a hasty promise to the fickle and vindictive spirits that always haunted such thresholds—a pledge of libations of fresh blood poured out upon the lintel in return for their protection. She counted to three. Bearing down white-knuckled on the handle, she pulled.

The door swung wide. There was a sudden rushing of air and a concussive crack like that of a whip. Antigone felt the entire weight of the blow hit her, falling squarely upon the precise juncture of bone where neck and back met. It knocked her facedown to the tiled floor. Her head rebounded with a hollow, almost musical tone.

In passing, the force plucked her off the ground again like a dried leaf and hurled her backward, tumbling end over end, down the corridor. She came to rest abruptly and jarringly against the wall. The darkness of oblivion swooped down upon her like a flock of black, predatory birds.

No. Can't black out now.

Willing healing blood to her badly battered—and, she realized with a peculiar calm detachment, probably broken—head and neck, she flailed wildly at the dark, smothering wings. She cast about for something, anything near at hand with which to beat them back.

Then, from somewhere within the press of smothering feathers and cruel talons, her hand closed upon something solid. She swung it at the murder of crows desperately, with both hands, with the remnant of her fading strength. Again and again.

Gradually, the voracious press of bodies began to withdraw from the field. At first singly and then in defiantly screaming squadrons they peeled away, leaving gaping holes, patches of glaring light in their wake.

The reflections from the mirrors lining the hall seemed unnaturally bright. As piercing and hurtful as sunlight. Her head throbbed and her hands ached from their deathgrip upon the…upon what? Antigone shook her head to clear it and instantly regretted doing so. The pain came crashing back, stronger then ever.

Already the delirium was fading, even the memory of it dwindling, retreating. She forced herself to focus, to remember. The object she had found, as if by chance (as if there were such a thing as chance in dreams and visions), had seemed a pole of some sort, or perhaps a staff. It was smooth and metallic, as cool to the touch as the copper of the door pull. And its head—its head was carved into a figure, a leering animal visage. It was the head of a jackal. The head of *the* Jackal. Anubis. The Guardian of the Pyramid. The laughing Warden of the Dead.

Antigone pushed herself unsteadily to her feet, wishing that the jackal-god had not withdrawn his talisman and his support so hastily. A crutch with which to lever herself up would have been most welcome right about now. She leaned heavily against the reflective surface of the wall to steady herself. In doing so, she inadvertently caught a glimpse of herself.

She was a fright. Her forehead was a mass of blood-matted hair that could not quite disguise the telltale hint of exposed bone beneath. Her entire head seemed cocked to one side, like that of a curious bird. Self-consciously, she drew up the cowl of her robe, only to find it decorated with angry streaks of fresh blood. She wiped at them, but smeared the garment further.

She tested her balance and, satisfied, struck out for the end of the corridor. As she approached the Hall of Audiences, she was relieved to find that the portal still stood ajar. She had feared the force of the concussion might have knocked it shut again.

Only a tatter of parchment, its edge curled and blackened, was still pinned beneath the blade of the ebon knife. With a rueful smile, she saw the splatter of fresh blood running down the doorjamb and filling the cracks on both sides of the sill. Her own blood. *One has to be very careful,* she thought, *what one promises the forgotten ones that dwell beneath thresholds.*

She stepped cautiously into the chamber, half-expecting to set off some new defensive warding. Her footfalls rang on the veined marble. Despite its imposing name, the Hall of Audiences was more a formal sitting room than a throne room. Most of the marble floor was covered with a rich, hand-woven rug rendered in the indigos and argents of the night sky. It depicted the Yggdrasil, the vast world-tree whose roots brooded in the nether regions and whose exultant branches pierced the very heavens. The earth was nothing more than a luscious fruit dangling from its boughs.

The piece was one of the great treasures of the Chantry of Five Boroughs. Delicate figures peeked from behind each leaf of the great oak, locked in the intricate Dance of Days. Antigone could pick out the individual tools of the craftsmen—miniature hammers, awls and lathes—as they bent over their work in single-minded concentration, working directly upon the living heartwood. She saw children chasing a ball through the tangled greenery, playing at draughts, knocking down lines of soldiers and snatching at those that tumbled from the bower out into the abyss.

The room's furnishings were ponderous; their tones, formal and languid. They clustered together in conspiratorial knots. Deep greens and cinnamons covered armchairs clearly designed to dwarf, if not utterly swallow, their occupants. A fieldstone fireplace covered most of one wall.

At the head of the chamber, seven marble steps formed a low dais. Their edges were squared, giving the feel of a ziggurat that had been pressed nearly flat. The raised platform was empty and unadorned, save for the regent's seal, which had been subtly and cunningly wrought into the very veins of the marble. White on white, the pattern was indistinguishable from any vantage save that of one kneeling upon the uppermost step. A flaming sword quenched in a cairn of stones.

There was no sign of the traditional throne or imposing high seat upon the dais. It was the regent's habit to greet her guests standing. She would quickly and precisely render the honors due to each according to his station, and then proceed immediately to the less formal and more intimate surroundings of the sitting area.

On these occasions, Sturbridge emerged from the forbidding, cave-like opening in the rear wall—a low, dark hole reminiscent of a crypt, peeking from beneath the dolmen arch of three monolithic granite slabs. The ancient, weathered menhirs were stacked upon each other in the form of the mathematical symbol for pi. They seemed to bear the entire weight of the chantry upon themselves.

Today, however, that burden fell on a different, more humble support. A Pillar of Smoke.

The floor at the foot of the dais had been cleared, the furnishings hastily shoved aside, the priceless rug rolled back as if it were of no account whatsoever. In their place, an intricate diagram of chalk and candlelight was inscribed on the marble floor.

Helena sat small and quiet in the center of that diagram, but defiantly held the position known as the Mountain Posture, one leg folded beneath her, the other knee proud and erect before her. It was a pose of vigilance and indomitable spirit. From it, the adept could weather the weight of the tons of rock pressing down upon her or be on her feet and in a fighting stance with a single fluid movement.

All of Helena's motions are fluid, Antigone thought enviously. Sturbridge called her chief of security "the Pillar of Smoke." Her counterpart, Johanus, was "the Pillar of Fire." Between the two, the adepts guided and protected the chosen.

Antigone saw immediately that all was not well. Helena was bent with weariness, her form gaunt and drawn with fatigue and bloodloss. Her entire body seemed to flicker uncertainly, like candle flame, as if a mere gust of wind would snuff out her tenuous existence.

The novice plucked up her courage and, pressing closer, forced as much bravado into her voice as she could muster. "You look like hell. You mind telling me exactly what's going on around here?"

Helena's voice, when it came, was broken and crackly, like static from an old radio receiver. "Nothing a little...hibernation won't cure. You look like you've gotten into...of a scuff, yourself. You okay?" She extended a hand tentatively. Antigone could see right through it.

She jerked back from Helena's touch, but almost immediately found herself leaning forward again, straining to pick out the fuzzy and missing words. "Jeez, Helena, I've seen ghosts healthier than you. How long since you've eaten anything?"

The flickering figure shrugged. "A week...maybe two...three. Can't just leave her.... Someone's got to..."

"Leave who? What are you talking about? There's nobody else here! Listen, I need your help. Can't you hear that damned alarm?"

Helena cocked her head to one side as if listening for a distant whisper. She nodded slowly, but otherwise made no move to assist. "How'd you...come by that...?" Helena looked as if she might reach out again.

Antigone's own hand went instinctively to her head. She felt fresh blood seeping from beneath the plaster of matted hair. "You had the door warded! And the communication node shut off. How were we supposed to get hold of you?!"

"You...weren't supposed to. The *noli te...intrare*? You walked...through that? Why didn't you just...?" Helena let the rest of her question trail off into the buzz of the static, seeing Antigone's embarrassment.

"Damn it, you know my background is in espionage, not your damned magical arts. I'm trying, okay?! Meanwhile, do you think you can break away for a minute and do something about the defensive-systems meltdown we've got going on out here?"

Helena smiled and shook her head. "My duty...here. Why don't you just...override the alarm and take...malfunctioning...system offline?"

"I'd love to. But only you and Sturbridge have got the clearance to override it. So are you going to help me, or am I going to have to go back in there and get her?"

"She can't... help you, Antigone. She's still... Here, I'm going to try...come out of this. I don't...if it can be done or not. Please...and step back a little."

"Please *what*?" Antigone echoed as, with one graceful motion, Helena rose to her feet and stepped forward, breaking the plane of the protective circle.

She immediately collapsed against Antigone, who stumbled backward before managing to catch her balance—barely keeping the adept from smashing face-first to the floor. "Enable communications node!" she bellowed toward the vaulted ceiling.

"Insufficient access," the defensive daemon's voice replied pleasantly. "Communications node locked by Helena, Adepta. Gimel-level clearance required to override."

"Emergency medical override."

There was a long pause. "Clearance confirmed. Communications node enabled. Emergency response team en route."

"You're a regular angel of mercy. Give me a systems status." Antigone rolled Helena onto her back. The adepta's entire body was convulsing violently. There was blood trickling from her nose and ears.

"Systems warning: Integrity failure. Location: Novice *domicilium*. Nature of failure: Dangerous degradation of spirit warding. Breach confirmed.

"Systems warning: Involuntary user-status change. Username: Diogenes, Salamander spirit attached to novice *domicilium*. Spirit binding breached. Spirit reclassified as renegade. Security clearance voided.

"Defensive systems warning: Intruder. Location: Novice *domicilium*. Number of intruders: One. Nature of intruders: Spirit entity, elemental. Unbound, violent.

"Defensive systems warning: Fire. Location: Novice *domicilium*. Depressurization sequence engaged. Depressurization sequence failure. Cause of failure: Local daemon offline; cannot initialize system."

Antigone cursed and interrupted the litany. "Any other users present in the novice *domicilium*?"

"Confirmed. Three novices present in *domicilium*. Emergency response team dispatched and on location. Team requesting reinforcement."

"Response team, report!" Antigone yelled, her words ringing overloud in the empty chamber. She knelt on Helena's shoulders in her attempt to pin the convulsing body. Antigone knew that, had Helena been in a right state of mind and able to focus her strength through the discipline of her martial training, the adepta would have tossed her aside effortlessly.

As it was, it was all Antigone could do to keep the flailing body from battering one or the other of them into oblivion. She kept losing her grip upon Helena and coming abruptly up against the floor as the adept flickered in and out of phase.

"Did someone call for a doctor?" Master Ynnis's voice sounded from directly behind her. She started and again lost her hold. Helena rolled and smashed into a low coffee table. The entire weight of the weathered stone slab of its surface, which seemed a sister of the famed Rosetta Stone, crashed down upon her.

Ynnis had an unsettling habit of entering a room without the formality of knocking or even of using the perfectly good doorways that had been provided for that purpose. He was an undisputed master of translocation. Judging from the discordant clamor that accompanied his entry, Antigone guessed he must have come by way of the pianoforte.

"Wretched thing is abysmally out of tune. What's the trouble here? Oh dear." He broke off suddenly seeing Helena again flicker momentarily out of existence, accompanied by the resounding crash of the stone that her body had, until that moment, been propping up.

"How long has she been like this?" Master Ynnis rummaged through the pockets of his robes and produced a paper fan. He snapped it open sharply, critically examining the masterfully understated brushwork of the painting and calligraphy that adorned it. Then he nodded and snapped it shut again. His long, triangular face, bobbing up and down, gave him the aspect of an ancient oracular serpent. "This will do nicely. The Chinese character signifies long life," he confided, handing the fan to Antigone.

"You want me to fan her?" she was openly incredulous.

"No, I would like for you to pry open her jaws and to wedge that between her teeth. With any luck, it will keep her from biting through her tongue. Or your fingers. How long?" he repeated his earlier question.

Antigone tried, with both hands, to wrestle the adept's mouth open. "I don't know. She's been fading in and out like that since I got here. Ten, maybe twenty minutes? But it only got bad when she stepped out of the circle. The seizure and the convulsions, I mean. I've just about got it now…. Damn it!" Helena flickered out again and Antigone nearly broke the fan in half against the floor.

Master Ynnis turned his attention to the circle that the novice had indicated. Its design was elegant in its simplicity. A circle of chalk and candlelight circumscribing a four-pointed star. The bottom point was easily three times as long as its fellows, giving it the aspect of a compass needle, or a cross, or perhaps a sword. There was something tantalizingly familiar about the shape of the diagram.

"Do you know where this leads?" he called to the struggling Antigone.

She didn't have the leisure to look up. "What do you mean, where it leads? And why hasn't that damned response team reported in yet? Got it!" She managed to insert the wooden handle of the fan between Helena's teeth. For a moment she feared the adept might bite right through it. "But won't the fan just fall out again, once she fades…? There she goes!"

"Excellent work," Ynnis said. "No, unless I am gravely mistaken, the fan should follow her. It is hers, after all. I removed it only now from a drawer on her bedside table that had been incautiously left open a crack. Anything of hers that she could not easily chew through would have sufficed. But I think it was an auspicious find, don't you? I asked where this *diagramma* leads only because it seems to me that the adepta is, at present, *between* places. She is quite literally neither here nor there. If I knew where 'there' was, I might attempt to bring her fully back 'here.' Or alternately to push her all the way through and out the other side. But as things presently stand—"

"Look, I'm way out of my depth here," Antigone interrupted. "Just tell me what I've got to do and I'll do it."

He seemed a bit flustered at her abrupt manner, but recovered himself gracefully. "Very well, as she comes back into phase, you will need to pin her down. She is far too weak. We will need to get some nourishment into her. Ready? Here she comes."

With one long tapering fingernail, he pressed a hole into the palm of his hand. A bead of crimson swelled and blossomed there. The fragrance of the rich vitae filled the room. Helena's lolling head turned instinctively toward it.

"She is so very pale." Ynnis pressed the cup of his hand to her lips. She sucked ravenously at the trickle of life, her tongue darting past the obstruction of the fan. Occasionally a drop would fall right through her insubstantial form, leaving a bright stain on the priceless carpet below.

"Well, that has put a touch of color back in your cheeks," Master Ynnis murmured. "I think that will stabilize your condition somewhat. Keep you from flying away from us entirely. Now if only we knew where you were so determined to be off to…"

"She's with Sturbridge," Antigone said. "She's got to be with Sturbridge. She kept saying that she couldn't leave her, that someone had to be there with her. I didn't realize what she meant. I thought she was just raving. The other end of that thing—that diagram—it's got to be in the regent's sanctum."

"Well, that should be an easy enough hypothesis to put to the test. If you will excuse me a moment…" He rose and turned toward the low door toward the inner sanctum.

"It's no good," Antigone called after him. "It's locked down tight. The security system… Damn, *that's* what the security system meant. It kept reporting that Helena was both in the Audience Hall and in the regent's sanctum."

Master Ynnis smiled and gave a slight bow. "Excellent. You have been most helpful. Now, if you will endeavor to keep hold of our little butterfly here, I will see if we cannot approach this problem another way."

He crossed the room, stepping carefully over the rolled end of the carpet. His slippered feet paused just outside the chalk line of the diagram. His eyebrows arched in surprise at what he found there.

"Have you had an opportunity to examine this *diagramma*?" he called to her. His words put her in mind of a conversation she had had with Helena in the crypts, when they had discovered Sturbridge's body. She struggled to keep her hold on the adepta. The infusion of blood may have stabilized her, but Helena seemed intent on burning her slight reserve of strength in the effort to dislodge Antigone.

"Yes, I mean, no. Not in any detail. Let me guess—an inverted circle. You're the damned expert. Why don't you tell me what it means."

He paused. "An inverted circle? Oh yes, I see. The rite does have some similarities to the Recursive Diagramma. A delightful insight." He paused. "You may have an affinity for geomantic abstractions. Yes, very promising, indeed."

"Lovely, another battery of pointless aptitude tests. Look, it's not like I don't appreciate the sentiment, but I'll save you some paper and me some further humiliation. It just doesn't click for me, okay? None of it. It's like trying to get blood from a stone."

He obviously was not familiar with the expression, as he appeared to give the problem some consideration. "One experiment at a time," he said at last. "First, the diagram. Then the aptitude testing—next Tuesday, the new moon, I should think. The blood from a stone had best be left to more experienced hands for the present. May I continue?"

Antigone only cursed under her breath and bore down on the struggling form in her grasp.

Ynnis circled the pattern, realigning a candle here, subtly altering a supporting glyph there. By the time he had come round full circle, he was satisfied that he had smoothed away the worst of the dangers inherent in the adept's ambitious and forbidden rite. By carefully altering the diagram, he had effectively disarmed it, rendering it nothing more than a mere circle of apportation.

Hopefully. With a smile, he closed his eyes, and stepped across the chalk line.

Chapter 11
Death Peeked Out of Him

Already Felton knew that something was amiss. He had been observing the southern entrance for just over twenty minutes now from the relative security of a coffee-shop doorway across the street and a few doors down. The Empire State Building was not an easy building to cover. It took up the entirety of a city block. It had four entrances, one facing in each direction. It was impossible to watch all of them at once. None of them should have been open at this hour.

For a building that was shut for the night, there was an awful lot of furtive activity taking place behind those glass-paned doors.

The briefing said that this was the ideal time and place for the hit, but Felton wasn't taking any chances. He had arrived well in advance of the target, to get the lay of the land and to see who else might be about tonight. All seemed pretty quiet, so far.

The dossier had been quite specific. The target was wont to come and go alone. He always used the southern entrance. And he would be very difficult to spot. Felton knew what that meant. There were a few of his fellow conspirators that fell into *that* category. He would have to take special precautions to ensure that his prey did not escape him unnoticed.

'Precautions' meant he would need a little time to work on that southern entrance, to safeguard it. Preferably unobserved.

He had been hanging back, making certain that none of the shadowy forms inside—apparitions that only rarely exposed themselves to the glare of the streetlight—were taking too close an interest in the scattered late-night revelers wandering past outside. If there were a guard posted within, he was either very good or very cavalier about his duties.

The fact that the target was a Nosferatu only made things challenging. Felton knew from his experience during the Sabbat occupation that these guys were just uncanny. There was no other way to describe it. There was this one guy on his squad about ten years back. They called him Ray, short for X-ray. Felton never knew the guy's real name. Funny, but there just never seemed any point in getting to know too much about the other guys on the squad. It only made you feel worse when one of your buddies finally bought it—went down and stayed down for good.

In hindsight, Felton didn't guess the guy much liked being called Ray, and didn't know why he had put up with it. They probably shouldn't have kept on him like that. How was the guy supposed to feel? If you were some kind of freak like that, you might be a little sensitive too.

It was his skin. It was the color and texture of Vaseline. It was not something that Felton was likely to forget, and it still gave him the creeps just thinking about it. If you caught Ray in a strong light, you could see right through the skin to his insides—the contracting muscles, the moist fatty layers, the voluminous coils of his guts. Ray kept his face covered most times. But Felton always found himself staring at him, trying to catch a peek of what lay beneath the loose rolls of fabric. When they shifted, you could see his skull, as clear as day. Ray carried the mark of his death with him everywhere. Felton snorted; he guessed everybody did. But with Ray, it was different. His death peeked out of him from the inside. It wore him like a clumsy and ill-fitting garment.

Sure, some of the guys grumbled, but Ray was something when it came to an infiltration. Felton had seen him walk right past guards like they weren't even there. Good men, too; not green recruits. And the damned thing was, he could even fool electronic surveillance systems. After one training session, Felton had reviewed the security tapes, just to see if he could pinpoint what it was that the Nossie was doing. But it was like he just wasn't there at all. That camera hadn't spotted him any more than the sentries had.

What Felton had come to learn, however, in working side-by-side with the elusive Nosferatu, was that, even where human and electronic means of observation failed, there was just no fooling the mechanical. Ray's unsettling abilities did not extend to breaking the basic principles of gravity, levers, counterbalance. A pressure plate would still sink under his weight. A tripwire would still break at his passing.

The device Felton had chosen for the task at hand this evening used just such a mechanical trigger—a small piece of metal, no larger than a toothpick. It was hinged at its center and designed to be placed across the gap in a pair of double doors, where it affixed magnetically. When either door opened, the hinge bent double, breaking a circuit and sending a signal to the radio earpiece he wore.

No amount of stealth could allow you to sneak past the mechanical trigger. Even if the Invisible Man himself were to open that door, Felton would know about it. The fact that he might not be able to see the figure slipping through the doorway was largely inconsequential. A sufficient volume of indiscriminate automatic-weapons fire, although sloppy, would get the job done.

All Felton had to do now was get close enough to set the device and get back to his hiding place without attracting any undue attention. He checked both Uzis slung under his threadbare greatcoat and, satisfied, struck out across the street.

There was a slight stagger to his step. His progress across the road was just a bit too slow and too parabolic for anything other than that of a late-night reveler. A bum, maybe. A wino. Reaching the recess of the southern entrance, he slapped at his pockets with both hands as if to assure himself that he still had his stash of money, and stooped to pick up something from the pavement.

"You'll want to move along. Now." The whisper seemed to come from directly behind him. The voice was bored, but carried an unmistakable rumble of threat. Felton had not heard even a hint of the speaker's approach.

Leaning heavily against the door as he straightened — so as to afford him the opportunity to position the device — Felton turned slowly to confront the newcomer. He held a palmed quarter up to the light of the streetlamp before stuffing it hastily into his pocket.

"I don't want your money, old man. On your way."

Felton smiled sheepishly and turned away. He tried to pick out the features of the shadowy figure without giving the other too good a look at him in return. He started up the sidewalk, feeling a presence at his back, keeping pace with him. He did not turn again, but started humming to himself. He had nearly reached the corner when he heard the high-pitched trilling in his ear. The signal.

Cursing, Felton spun back toward the doors, but came to an abrupt halt, face-to-face with his shadow. A firm grip took hold of his elbow and steered him back toward the corner. "I said, move along."

Felton took one stumbling step and fell heavily against his escort. The other, in turn, slumped heavily against the wall. As Felton wheeled away from him, the hilt of an oversized hunting knife could be seen protruding from the felled man's chest.

"Be back for you in just a second," Felton whispered, although whether he addressed the man or the abandoned knife was unclear. He sprinted back down the block toward the entrance, but already he knew he was too late. The electronic chirping in his ear had fallen silent. The doors had already closed again. His target was inside.

Felton cursed. He deliberated only a second, his gaze flickering back and forth from the body left in plain view at the corner and the door where his target had just disappeared. If he dragged the body into the cover of a nearby doorway, he might be able to avoid detection for a while longer. He might be able to take up his post again and wait for the target to reemerge. But there was always the chance that some patrol car might come across the remains propped in the doorway, or the not-inconsiderable puddle of blood on the sidewalk out front of the Empire State Building. That would attract all kinds of unwanted attention, not the least of which from the police helicopter that now banked uncomfortably close by.

It took only a moment to make up his mind. His earpiece chirped again as he burst through the double doors into the dimly lit interior. His boots rang loudly on the tiled floor. The noise was compromising, but speed was of the essence now. And at least the heavy footfalls would cover the sound of his drawing and readying the twin Uzis. If there were any sentries left inside, they were about to earn their combat pay.

Up ahead, Felton heard the telltale chime of the elevator doors opening. He sped around the corner but was only halfway down the long empty hall when the doors sighed shut. Too late again.

He skidded to a stop and pounded furiously on the 'up' button. He had one more chance to trap his prey—assuming, of course, that Emmett was taking the elevator all the way up to the eighty-sixth floor.

Felton didn't know why the elevators didn't go beyond the eighty-sixth floor. Maybe that was as high as they could safely build them back in those days. Where this bank of elevators topped out, it opened up onto a short, narrow stretch of hallway leading to a single elevator car. During the daytime, it ferried a steady stream of tourists to and from the observation deck.

That narrow access corridor would be a perfect killing field. In the confined space, there would be nowhere to escape the deadly hail of bullets.

Felton again pounded on the elevator button and cursed. When would one of those blasted cars come? He felt exposed here, standing before the bank of elevators. He glanced hastily down the corridor in both directions and became suddenly aware of the security camera just above him.

Well, if they didn't know he was here by now, they would soon. Neither of the other two elevators seemed to be moving. Locked down for the night, he thought. He saw the elevator that Emmett had taken pause at the eighty-sixth floor and then start its descent. There would be no way to catch him now. Not anywhere short of the observation deck itself. And Felton had reason to believe that Emmett would not be alone there.

He smiled, thinking of the reaction he would get if he returned to report that he had taken out not only the target, but the prince himself in the bargain. His smile quickly vanished. He had no doubt that his co-conspirators—as much as they railed against Calebros's oppression and his criminal neglect of his duties—would not hesitate to sacrifice Felton to escape the backlash that would follow upon the heels of such a high-profile assassination.

Felton didn't much relish the thought of trying to face down two competent Nosferatu single-handed either. You had to assume that one of them would always be behind you, and that made things tricky.

Even before the elevator had reached the lobby, he had again changed gears and resignedly turned, trotting off toward the western entrance. It wouldn't do to call too much attention to the southern door. Best to make it seem that he had just followed the target in that way. He could circle around, conceal the body lying outside, and take up his observation post again. Just to see if another opportunity presented itself. All might not yet be lost.

As he approached the western doors, he was certain he was being scrutinized very closely. If there were unseen observers, however, the guards showed enough discretion not to challenge him or the deadly array of firepower that he leveled at every movement—real or imagined—in the shadows.

He had no sooner slipped through the double doors into the relative safety of the outside air, when a resounding concussion shook the entire building.

Looking up, Felton saw a wave of fire break from the upper floors, blossoming out in all directions. It took an effort of will to wrest his gaze away, to force his body to move. He shook himself and broke into a run.

He was already a block away when the first shrapnel of glass, steel and concrete began to rain down upon the pavement.

The explosion must have deafened him, because he was only gradually becoming aware of the incessant chirping in his ear. Angrily, he scooped out the receiver and crushed it underfoot. One thought and one thought only kept playing itself over and over again in his mind.

The Empire State Building has just been blown up. He repeated it aloud, but it did no good. The statement simply refused to take root upon his mind. He had witnessed the explosion, but there was something inherently unreal about it. Skyscrapers don't just blow up.

Somebody has to blow them up. This second thought was more disturbing than the first. Who would want to blow up the Empire State Building? And why? If it was just some kind of whacked-out terrorist stunt, why not blow it up in broad daylight, when you would be sure to get a whole slew of tourists thrown into the bargain? More bang for your buck?

Unless, of course, the target would not be there during the daylight. That thought stopped him altogether. The target. *His* target. Emmett. He wondered if Emmett had been caught in that explosion. Perhaps his mission had not ended in failure after all. He could not return at this point to try to confirm the kill. That would be insane. But why the hell would you blow up a national landmark just to kill one Nosferatu? It was overkill. It just didn't make any sense, unless…

Unless it wasn't Emmett that you were trying to kill. Felton's thoughts immediately went to the prince. Would it be worth the reprisals, the backlash, the media exposure, the Masquerade breach of blowing up such a famous landmark to kill the prince? Felton's associates certainly would not think so. The cost was far too high for them to pay. But perhaps there were others who felt differently. Or perhaps they would feel differently if they were certain that they would not be the ones left to settle the tab.

Felton followed this thread of inquiry through labyrinthine passages—all of which led him toward the same unavoidable conclusion. It was the most disturbing thought of all. It broke over him with a cool certainty that drowned what should have been the rising fire of panic within him.

He had been set up.

Chapter 12
The Petulance of Kings and Emperors

"There is only one thing further, my lord. The matter of your legate to the colonials." Doktor Frederic Lohm had hoped to sound nonchalant. He winced at the effect his words produced. The perpetually damp, rough-hewn walls of the crypts parroted his words back to him. His very footfalls as he hurried after his master sounded clumsy and scurrying. The sputtering torches flanking the ominous ironbound door just ahead snorted derisively, mocking him.

It had never been his privilege to pass beyond that notorious portal—the most feared threshold in all of Vienna— but Herr Doktor was under no illusions as to what lay beyond. It was that damnable cell. Its very proximity always made him ill at ease. There was something in the air here, a miasma. A malaise. It was not something that you could put a finger on. The enigma resisted his best efforts to define, measure, document and analyze. It rebuffed all the most systematic probings of *sciencia et sophia*. But the fact remained that centuries of torpor and torment took their toll upon a place.

The subterranean vault was not a cell in the sense of a prison or dungeon. Or at least, not entirely so. Upon reflection, Herr Doktor was forced to admit that one of the infamous chamber's most significant functions *was* to keep a uniquely dangerous and perverse intellect isolated from the society of lesser beings—upon whom it was his habit to prey.

But no, the chamber was certainly more of a cell in the monastic sense. A hermitage. A place where one might retreat from the demands of this world and sink into the solace of solitude, prayer and contemplation. The cell's occupant was widely believed to have spent literally centuries here, in the deep rejuvenative torpor which is the balm of those weary in body and spirit.

At the door, Etrius, the heir of House Tremere and the leader of the Council of Seven, turned. He paused, one hand upon the imposing iron door pull. The room's wardings were of such potency and antiquity that, if they had ever been rendered in such fleeting and ephemeral media as mere paint or blood, time had since completely erased all evidence of such transitory markings. The glyphs that now covered the portal were etched into the very surface of the blackened wood and filled with molten silver. It might have been only a trick of the torchlight, but the runes seemed to be constantly in motion, flowing liquidly one into another.

Doktor Lohm shivered involuntarily. He could not fathom what his master saw in this place. No, that was not precisely true, he knew exactly what his master came here to see. What the good doktor could not fathom was what drove Etrius to keep returning to such a place, night after night. Better by far to let such things lie undisturbed.

"Yes, yes," Etrius was clearly impatient and distracted, his mind already caught up in anticipation of the familiar opening tones of the dark fugue that awaited him within. "What news of the legate?"

"Well, that is just it, my lord. There is no word from the legate. It has been some weeks since his last report. I fear for his safety."

"They would not dare." Etrius pronounced each word separately and distinctly. Lohm had served his master long enough that he could not fail to recognize that the low rumble was not intended merely as a threat to the upstart colonials. It was also a very personal warning. He understood clearly that the current line of speculation would not fall upon welcome ears. He must tread carefully, here.

"Certainly not, my lord. But surely if the ambassador were well he would have reported in. As was not only his duty, but his habit."

Etrius visibly struggled for patience. His gaze locked upon that of the good doktor and bore down. But the other was unflinching. Etrius recognized the long-suffering look of one who had been trained from an early age to weather the petulance of kings and emperors. He recalled that, in the doktor's youth, he had been raised to serve as a personal secretary to the Kaiser Franz-Josef, a posting in which he had served with distinction.

Etrius exhaled slowly and deliberately, surrendering his hold upon the door pull. "You have made inquiries, of course?"

"I have received…unsatisfactory replies from the chantry house." He drew back just short of the phrase "outright forgeries"—the accusation that first leapt to his lips. Given the master's present mood, it was best to refrain from such inflammatory rhetoric.

"What account do they offer for the legate's sudden silence?"

"They say he is wounded, my lord, that he has slipped into torpor after wounds heroically suffered during the liberation of New Yor—that is to say, New Amsterdam."

"Ah, New Amsterdam!" Etrius's eyes focused on some dim point in the middle distance, lost in an inner reverie. His tone held a note of longing or regret that caught the good doktor unawares.

"Have you ever been to the colonies, my lord?" Lohm asked, doubtful and puzzled. He found himself wondering what images could possibly be playing themselves out upon the inner surface of his master's skull. He imagined it would be a peculiar juxtaposition of buggies drawn by steam-powered horses and ziggurats of steel and concrete clamoring with unbridled ambition toward the moon.

Etrius was not "out of touch" *per se*. Certainly not in the way that so many elders had grown—shying away from all traffic with modern technology and culture. It was more that he grasped all new advances in terms of what for him was the primary paradigm. His worldview was firmly grounded in the rigors of the great medieval university system. His intellect had been nurtured on the disciplines of the Trivium and Quadrivium—the pillars of a proper classical education. His keen mind was further tempered in the fires of the numerous secret intellectual societies of the age. With the passion of youth, he had ravenously delved into the arts forbidden, arcane, gnostic, alchemical and heretical.

A man who had grown accustomed to instant communication with colleagues as far removed as the Universities of Paris and Padua—a full six hundred years before the birth of a certain Mr. A. Graham Bell—was not going to have any difficulties with the principle of the telephone. It was just that it might not be exactly the same principle that everyone else grasped. Lohm had, on one memorable occasion, seen his master actually banish an entire coven of "weird sisters" (by which he meant, trans-sisters and re-sisters) from a troublesome radio receiver.

"New Amsterdam?" Etrius seemed to come reluctantly back to himself. He bent visibly under the renewed weight of his responsibilities. "No, I have never been there in the flesh. But I have...I have heard such intriguing stories. Who is our regent in the colony now? Or is Meerlinda still guiding the growth of the chantry house there personally?"

The doktor suppressed a smile. "No, my lord. The councilor has recently delegated that duty—sometime in the last century or two. I am uncertain of the exact date, but I will look it up for you when I return to the library."

Etrius looked somewhat wistful and disappointed. He waved aside the doktor's offer. "Do not trouble yourself. It is of no matter. I should think it must have been difficult for Meerlinda to give it up. Who is the new regent?"

"Aisling Sturbridge, my lord. You will recall that Ms. Sturbridge is the one who served us with such distinction and discretion in the matter of—"

"Ah, yes. Sturbridge. Such a promising young lady. I am pleased to see that she has done so well for herself."

"But there still remains the small matter of the ambassador's health. And the murders..." Lohm prompted.

"I should have thought that the legate would have concluded this business of investigating the murders before rashly wading out into the thick of battle. Was his report in this matter—how did you put it?—unsatisfactory as well?"

"You are quite correct on both counts, my lord. I find the ambassador's alleged behavior difficult to account for. It is my opinion that he should be recalled as soon as he may be safely transported, that we might make more direct inquiries into this matter."

"An eminently sensible suggestion. I must admit that I am tempted to send along my personal physician to attend upon our fallen hero and speed him back to us."

At this the doktor did laugh aloud. "You shall not escape me that easily, my lord. It is quite unthinkable that I should abandon my post at such a time." His voice dropped to the firm tones of one confiding an unwelcome prognosis. "If I may speak frankly, you have not been yourself since this latest ill-considered voyage to Mexico Cit—that is to say, Tenochtitlan. I am disturbed by the malaise that has taken hold of you these nights.

"I further believe," the doktor anticipated and forestalled interruption, "that the humours of this foul dungeon are producing a singularly detrimental effect upon you. What is to be gained by coming here each night and spending all of your waking hours within that cell? Nothing. Nothing certainly that is more important than your health and good judgment. We, this House, can ill afford to sacrifice either of these assets upon the altar of your present obsession. If He has not told you that already, He is doing you—and all of His House—a great disservice."

Etrius put a hand upon Lohm's shoulder, but whether in reassurance or simply out of weariness, it was impossible to determine. "He doesn't speak to me anymore," he confided. "At all."

Already, Lohm knew that his master was lost to him. Etrius turned his back and recrossed the distance to the ominous rune-carved door.

"Then why are you doing this?" the doktor called after him. "You don't have to put yourself through this, you know. He won't think any less of you. Surely there can be no doubt of your devotion...."

Etrius half-turned. "He doesn't even know that I am here," he said simply. "I'm not even sure what He would think if He did know."

Lohm took a single awkward step forward. "Master, I..."

But Etrius interrupted him. "You will send in the Astors, if you will not go yourself. Leave me now."

Lohm recognized that tone. It brooked no further argument. "Yes, my lord. Your will be done. But you must make at least a token effort to take care of yourself. If you will not, then there is no place for me here. I will not remain to suffer through the indignity of being ignored, only to win certain disgrace when my warnings prove to be all too accurate. You are all that is left to us; you need to stop squandering the remaining resources of this House."

Etrius managed a sad smile. "Are your medicines always so bitter? I will confide a secret to you, Doktor. This place, this is the only place I know of, the only place I have ever found, where I can—if only for the flicker of a single night—be free of the never-ending procession of demands and entreaties; of supplications and intrigues; of feints and fronts; of attacks and assassination attempts. Do you know what I call this place? I call it the Asylum. Here, only the thinnest of barriers—this very door—stands between the rest of the world and unutterable bedlam. It is only when I enter into this cell, when I fasten the latch firmly behind me, that I am at last free from the ever-present wailing of the afflicted."

"Now you are having a small jest at my expense, yes? Are my words, also, nothing more than the bayings of a madman to you? You know what is commonly said of the man who finds all of his fellow men mad?"

Etrius smiled. Unbearable weariness peeked through the crack in his facade. "Tomorrow night," he said. "You may call upon me in my study. But bring me remedies that are a bit more palatable. Goodnight, Doktor."

Lohm bowed resignedly and backed away three paces before straightening, as prescribed by protocol. "Goodnight, my lord."

Etrius watched the doctor walk the length of the corridor and turn the corner. Only when he heard the outer door fasten did he turn his attentions back to the cell. The wardings did not stop or stay him. They had grown accustomed to his touch.

He closed the door behind him and leaned heavily against it. There was silence within and a great sense of what Etrius could only describe as *absence*. It was the same absence one might feel in walking into the room of a child who had just passed away. All of the signs were there—the disarranged clothes, the scattered playthings—but the spirit, the meaning, had gone out of the symbols. Now they spoke only of absence.

Etrius crossed to the stone bier, the room's only furnishing, and knelt before it. For centuries, this had been the resting-place of his master—Tremere, the Founder of this House. Now it lay empty. Etrius pressed his forehead to the cool stone and let the weight of his thoughts leach out directly through the rock. A single broken sob escaped the remains of his atrophied lungs. A wrenching, animal wail. But whether he mourned for his master, or for his House, or for himself, he no longer knew. The boundaries had long ago blurred about the edges and his old eyes—now filmed over with cataracts of blood—could no longer make out such fine distinctions.

Chapter 13
Ice, Blood and Laudanum

Ynnis stepped out into a scene of carnage. Entire shelves of carefully arranged books had been overturned, their contents strewn haphazardly about the room. The monitor from the bedside computer desk had precipitated to the floor, its face shattered and throwing sparks. A nearly bloodless body thrashed on the floor. Another lay insensate on the bed, an attitude of undisguised terror and torment seared into its features.

He shivered involuntarily as he approached the bedside. The regent's sanctum was as cold as a meat locker. Icicles hung like drapes from the cast-iron rails of the canopied bed. The bed curtains themselves had been torn down, wadded up into a great, bloodstained ball, and cast into a corner.

Tripping over a toppled tripod, Ynnis came down heavily, his knee smashing an empty bell jar rolling slowly across the slick floor. He felt glass bite flesh. He managed to catch himself on the edge of the bed, but found his face coming abruptly up against that of the corpse still tangled in the sheets.

Sturbridge.

One white-knuckled fist was knotted in the bedclothes. The other was frozen in the act of clawing at the glistening spike protruding from her chest.

Master Ynnis bent closer to examine the curious implement that impaled his regent. It was a long crimson shard of ice. A multifaceted crystal of frozen blood, driven through her heart. As he watched, a slow trickle of life condensed, slipping down the side of the spike and sliding down the curve of her breast.

Cautiously, he extended a finger to the ruby bead. He felt it give slightly beneath his touch and then cling fast as he withdrew his hand. Pressing fingertip to tongue, he closed his eyes and rolled the droplet around in his mouth.

"Laudanum," he said aloud, his breath issuing forth in a frosty red-tinged cloud. "And enough of it to kill a modest herd of elephants." He turned his attention to the second body still thrashing about on the floor. "And what can you tell us about all this, I wonder." He recognized her features instantly. It was Helena. Or at least some flickering remnant of the adepta. He laid a firm hand upon her to still her flailings, but there was little enough substance remaining to her. His hand passed through her as if she were a phantasm.

"Open communications node," he whispered. "Emergency medical override. Ynnis, Maestro."

"Clearance confirmed. Communications node enabled."

"Antigone, can you hear me?" he asked.

"Thank God. I read you. Did you...find her?" There was only the briefest of hesitations in her voice.

"Indeed. Please listen carefully. The adepta's situation is most critical. There are, unfortunately, some very sound practical reasons why the bilocation ritual is forbidden."

"The bilo what?

"Bilocation. The good adepta was endeavoring to sustain a ritual that would allow her to exist simultaneously in two places at the same time. It is a misguided adaptation of the standard apportation rite that was first documented by Goratrix back in the..."

"That's great, really. I'm looking forward to hearing all about it. But these convulsions are getting worse. She's shaking now, shaking like her body's trying to pull itself apart. And the blood's just streaming out of her mouth and nose and ears and...and I think I'm losing her here."

"Stay calm. You're not going to lose her. I'm going to attempt to push her back through to you. Here's what you need to do. Are you all right?"

"Damn it, I'm not the one that's dying here! What do I need to do?"

"First of all, you must pin her down. If I succeed, the adepta is likely to come off the floor like a rocket. She's still going to be deep in the seizure. But whereas before she was only struggling with about fifty percent of her strength..."

Antigone groaned. "I get the idea."

"Excellent. Your primary job is to get her through those first moments without her killing herself. Can you handle that?"

"I think so. What happens after those first few moments?" Antigone asked.

"Then she will most likely try to kill you," he said. "The convulsions will recede, leaving the Beast firmly in control—the ravaging animal instincts to fight and feed."

"So what are we supposed to do about that?"

"I would suggest that, once you are absolutely certain that the adepta has revived, you incapacitate her as quickly as possible."

"I'm sure I don't need to remind you that Helena is an Adept? I've seen her damned near tear a Tzimisce shovel-head limb from limb with nothing more than her voice! I'm just a novice here, remember?"

"The adepta will be deep in the clutches of the Beast. She shouldn't have the concentration or composure to invoke any of the truly horrific blood magics. That should prove some small comfort."

"I could see where you might think that," she said. "So I just take out the chantry's head of security—and, incidentally, its martial-arts instructor—in a one-on-one fight, right? Any good reason why I can't just cold-cock her now?"

"If you were to incapacitate her in her current condition, you would surely sever the remaining connection and our best hope of getting her back in one piece. I suggest employing a heavy blunt object, preferably to the back of the head or neck. And *only* when you're absolutely certain that she is whole again."

"You sound like you've done this sort of thing before," she accused.

There was a long pause. "Never successfully."

Antigone shifted her hold slightly and squirmed around to where she was within easy reach of a stout wooden table leg that had, until recently, supported the onyx slab of the coffee table.

"All right," she called uncertainly. "I'm ready if you're ready."

Master Ynnis made no answer. He rubbed his hands together slowly as if for warmth. As he did so, the flesh of his fingers grew translucent, revealing luminescent knobs of bone within. He crossed to the still-struggling body on the floor and placed one hand steadyingly upon her chest. The other he raised high as if in invocation. When he curled it into a fist, one could almost hear the clacking of the exposed bones folding together.

He knew what must surely follow, but it was better that Antigone should not. It was no small matter to rejoin a splintered existence. Nor one to be undertaken lightly.

With a great shout, he slammed the fist down upon Helena's heart. Her entire body bucked under the weight of the blow. Again the fist rose and fell, hitting her with all the raw force of an electrostat. He raised his fist a third time.

The third blow fell. The flickering blue form shredded, flying like tattered shadows to the four corners of the room.

Master Ynnis collapsed upon the floor from his exertion, the fist so recently raised against the adepta clutching at his own chest. He was not a young man when he was first cast into this benighted existence, flickering between the worlds of the living and the dead. He had carried his infirmities with him across that threshold.

The lights in the room had receded to dim pinpricks. A sharp, shooting agony raced the entire length of his left side, following the disused conduit of vestigial veins and arteries. His face contorted and curled up at the edges, taking on the aspect of the monstrous death mask it should rightly have assumed years ago. His ears filled with the roar of blood. The pounding of the surf. The inevitable progression of the tides, locked in epic battle, hurling themselves wave after wave against the heel of the mountains.

Chapter 14
Don't Tease the Dogs

Felton paused just down the block from the familiar rundown building. He was halfway there before he realized where his feet had been taking him. If he had sat down to deliberate what he should do next, he probably would never have come. But where else was he going to go? Since the dramatic events earlier this evening, there was no telling who he could trust any longer.

The old building leaned perceptibly to the right. It looked as if it had at some point been divided up into three or four apartments. Felton, however, knew that there was only one resident at present. He stood a long time, watching to make sure that there was no one else on the street at this hour who might observe his movements, or worse, try to interfere. Cautiously, he approached the front stoop. He climbed the stair and tried to press himself into the shadow of the doorway. There were four bells to chose from (three of them still lit), so he mashed them all. Then came the waiting.

It was broken by the unmistakable pump of a shotgun.

"Who the hell is it? And while you're at it, you might tell me why I shouldn't just blow you and this door all over the street?"

Felton's own voice was a pitched whisper. "Charlie, it's me. I'm...I'm in trouble. I need your help."

The voice on the other side quieted and cursed. "You alone?"

"Yeah, you could say that," Felton replied with a lame attempt at a laugh. He could not remember when he had felt more alone.

"Didn't realize it was a funny question. You alone or not?"

"Yes! There's no one else here. Now open up before somebody sees me here."

That seemed to get through to Charlie. If Felton was in trouble, it wouldn't do for him to be seen here—even if Charlie turned him away flat. A deadbolt slid back, then a chain, then another bolt. The door opened a crack.

Felton slipped inside and closed the door quickly behind him. When he turned, he found himself looking down the double barrel of the shotgun. Charlie stood protectively between him and the four motorcycles that crowded the downstairs hallway. A stairway on the left led up to Charlie's place.

"So talk," he said. Charlie had hastily thrown on his worn leather jacket as an afterthought. His chest was bare and his stomach hung down a bit over the lip of his jeans. The jacket was riddled with odd bits of metal, and even his shaggy mustache stuck out at strange angles.

"You won't need that, buddy," Felton replied, nodding toward the gun.

"Prove it to me."

Very slowly, Felton pulled open his coat, revealing the Uzis. He carefully unbuckled them and laid them on the floor.

"Anything else?" Charlie prompted.

Felton reached for his knife, only to realize that he had left it buried in the chest of a guard outside the Empire State Building.

"I lost my knife in the scuffle. Look, Charlie, something awful has happened. I…"

"I know. It's all over the news. You hurt?" The shotgun never wavered, belying the note of concern in his question. Felton thought he could pick out the crackle of voices upstairs from the emergency newscast. Live coverage, no doubt. The place must be swarming with cops and camera crews by now.

"Look, I didn't blow up the…"

"Shhh." Charlie cut him off sharply with a painful prod of the shotgun to the ribs. The aging biker jerked his head sharply to one side as if to indicate the neighbors just beyond the wall and the fact that he did not care to be overheard. "We'll talk upstairs. You go on up first."

"Whatever you say, Charlie. I'm glad you were in. I didn't know where else to go."

"You should have called. I would have told you where to go."

Felton laughed off the threat. "I didn't know you even had a phone, much less the number."

"It would have been better if you never even knew where this place was. How'd you find me?"

Felton reached the top of the stair. There were two apartments off the hall and the door to the first was standing open. The only light from inside was the flickering blue of the television screen. Felton hesitated in the doorway. The reek of old blood and motor oil was nearly overwhelming.

"You'll have to pardon the mess. I wasn't expecting company. Clear yourself some space on the sofa. I'm sure you'll be on again in a minute. I've got to check on the dogs."

Charlie disappeared into an unlit back room. Something clanged and Felton heard his host curse and then begin muttering angrily to himself. Felton listened intently, straining to pick out the telltale click of a telephone receiver. Nothing. Just the steady invective, some rooting around in the dark, a lonesome animal moan and the rattling of chains.

Relieved, Felton picked his way around the bike that was the present object of Charlie's obsession, It dominated the near part of the room, spread out in the midst of a rebuild. It was a bruiser of a machine, a custom job. The seat towered nearly as high as Felton's shoulder. He doubted whether he could have even mounted this monster without standing on something. The high-backed chopper seat was draped in a tight-fitting runner of long human bones, bound together in parallel with copper wire.

Felton picked his way carefully around the bike and over the detached muffler and tailpipe that lay nearby. He accidentally kicked a handful of nuts and bolts, scattering them across the room. Not everything underfoot, however, rolled away so easily or rang of metal. From the stench that rose up from the softer, more clinging bits, Felton guessed that his host had been recently harvesting more adornments for his bike. Well, perhaps not *very* recently.

Felton was at a loss for words. "Damn, Charlie," he called. "I mean…just *damn*."

Charlie reemerged, grinning wide, proud. "You like her? Been working on her for the better part of three months."

"What can I say?" Felton stammered. "I've never seen anything like it. You do this…often?"

"Same as breathing—every chance I get." This thought struck Charlie as particularly funny and he nearly hollered with laughter. "You get it? Breathing!"

"Yeah, breathing. That's a good one, buddy." Felton tentatively flipped up the sofa cushion, dislodging its contents directly onto the floor rather than risk touching them with his hands. Turning the cushion over, he replaced it and sat down.

The TV rested on a long packing crate whose dimensions were disturbingly reminiscent of a coffin. On screen, the picture showed a panning aerial view of the Empire State Building. A floor about four-fifths of the way to the top was still wreathed in flames. Felton leaned closer. "You mind if I turn it up?"

"Fine by me. Louder is better. That way there's less chance that the neighbors will overhear anything you might have to say." Charlie crossed behind him and again left the room. A bright stab of light from the refrigerator lit up just enough of the kitchen to ensure Felton that he did not want to see any more of it.

"You want a beer?" his host called.

"Thanks, but all this has kind of put me off the stuff," Felton said.

Charlie popped open two cans, one after the other, without ever letting go of the shotgun. It was lowered, at least, when he returned. As far as Felton was concerned, that was a marked improvement. Charlie shoved the two cans toward his guest. They were stacked one on top of the other, with his big ruddy fist wrapped around the middle. "Wait till you see these pictures. They'll put you right back on the stuff. You might have smiled for the camera at least."

The picture cut to the internal security camera. It showed a remarkably clear, if unflattering, black-and-white shot of Felton. From this angle, he was all balding forehead and brandished submachine guns. As he watched himself, he angrily pounded the elevator call button and then, plain as day, caught sight of the camera and rolled his eyes.

Charlie nearly sprayed his beer across the screen. "You know, it was funny just watching it. But it's even funnier watching *you* watch it." He wiped one forearm across his nose and mouth and snorted robustly. "So that was it, huh? The mission. To blow up the damned Empire State Building. Just like that. Jeez, I can't believe you did it. You!"

"What's that supposed to mean, 'you can't believe it was me'? It wasn't me! I didn't do anything. Just wound up in the wrong place at the wrong time."

"Uh, right. Sure you did, buddy. If that's the line you want to take with old Charlie, that's fine. But, would you look at the time! It's been real nice of you to stop by. Good luck to you on your mission and all that. Can't wait to hear how it all turns out." Charlie prodded him in the shoulder with the business end of the shotgun.

Felton calmly pushed the barrel aside. "No. I'm serious, Charlie. Look, I've got the mission briefing right here. You can read it yourself. At this point, I just don't care anymore. I've got nothing more to lose."

Very slowly, he reached under his coat, painfully aware of the cool metal of the shotgun now pressing unambiguously against the side of his head. There was a threatening growl from the back room and a rattling of chain. Felton drew out a rolled-up manila envelope from an inside pocket and held it out.

Reluctantly, Charlie took the envelope in his free hand and lowered the gun. He crossed to put the bulk of the monstrous bike between himself and his guest, spreading the dossier out on the high seat. The shotgun rested upon the seat as well, not aimed at Felton, but still pointed in his direction, the trigger within easy reach.

Charlie flipped through the pages of the mission briefing, grumbling to himself. "A hit, huh? I've got to hand it to you buddy, you don't do anything halfway, do you? If it was me now, I'd probably have stuck with the old standby. Sniper's rifle. Quick, reliable, no entanglements. Demolitions are always imprecise, not to mention messy. Hell, did you even bag the target?"

"I don't know. I mean, no! I didn't get off a shot. It was all a set-up. Somebody blew up the god-damned building!" He gestured emphatically toward the TV as if the newscaster would jump in to back him up.

Charlie shook his head and closed the folder in disgust. He waved it at his guest accusingly. "How the hell did you think you were going to get away with something like this? Didn't you know there would be national press coverage? It's a freaking national landmark. Shit, man, you're going to have the F.B. fucking I. all over your sorry, worm-eaten ass. You've got a lot of nerve waltzing in here after pulling a stunt like this! I've got a good thing going here—a place of my own, a little restoration business on the side. And I'm doing all right for myself. For the first time in I can't tell you how long, I'm doing all right. I'm not about to pull up stakes and blow town because of you bringing the heat down on me here."

"You're not listening to what I'm telling you!" Felton bellowed, pushed himself up off the sofa. He started toward his host, one hand raised to emphasize his point. But he broke off with a curse and just turned his back on Charlie. "Look, I was set up. I didn't even have any explosives. Nothing like *that*!" He gestured toward the TV, which was presently showing a tight shot of a rather horse-faced anchorwoman. "Forget it! It's not worth it. I thought I could count on you. After all the shit we've been through, I thought... Just forget it. Thanks for the beer."

He slammed the untouched beer down on top of the TV. A jet of foam shot up, only to fall back again, streaking the screen with bright, multicolored beads of light. Felton started angrily for the door.

A burly hand planted firmly in the center of his chest stopped him. His host's other hand still clenched down upon the rolled manila folder, smashing its center into a tangle. Felton noted that the shotgun still rested on the bike seat. This fact came as some small comfort but, given the close quarters and the intensity of his adversary, Felton didn't like the thought of going hand to hand with the larger man either.

Still, broken bone and cartilage healed faster than the carnage wrought by a shotgun blast.

"Look at me, damn you," Charlie barked. Felton met his gaze evenly. "You blow up that building?"

"Damn it, Charlie! You know I didn't..."

"I didn't ask you what I knew. I asked if you blew up the building. Now quit squirming and answer the damned question. Yes or no?"

Felton choked off an angry retort. He fumed. "No."

Charlie held his gaze a long time, sizing him up. At last he broke the silence. "Then what the hell are you so defensive about?" At the word, "hell," he gave Felton a shove that sent the other reeling backward toward the open door of the back room.

Felton's heel caught on the exhaust pipe, sprawling him flat out on his back. There was a wet, throaty growl directly at his ear. Felton instinctively rolled, came to his knees and then started backpedaling away from the shadowy recess. Two pairs of fierce eyes, luminous with the reflected flickering blue of the TV, followed him. For a moment he thought he could pick out the halo of a tangled mane around the nearest set of eyes. The long, greasy black hair draped to the floor, barely concealing the sharp angular jut of pink, hairless shoulders beneath. Wickedly clawed and five-fingered talons jutted forward, palms planted firmly on the floorboards. And the hint of softer, distinctively feminine curves, ill-concealed, just beyond the snarled cascade of hair.

Chain rattled across the wooden floor, snapped taut and held. A wild, purely animal baying broke from the darkness as the beast strained against its tether. But whatever Charlie had chained up in the back room, they were certainly not dogs. At least, they hadn't started out life that way. There was no telling what they might or might not be now.

A rough hand grabbed Felton by the shoulder and plucked him effortlessly from the floor. He found himself spun around and then the motion was just as suddenly arrested by a meaty slap. Both of Felton's arms were caught in a vise-like grip and pinned to his sides. Charlie bent over him, leaning directly into his face. His words reeked of stale beer and cigarettes. Felton thought that this was surely it. That the big man was about to snap him cleanly in half like a twig.

"Don't. Tease. The. Dogs!"

"Sorry," Felton whispered. "Sorry. Look, Charlie, I shouldn't have come. It was wrong to put upon you like this. It's just that this whole damned town has turned pretty hostile all of a sudden and I thought...I thought it might be, well, different here."

"Hostile is right. The damned Sabbat occupation is nothing compared to what you're up against now, partner." Phrases like "manhunt," "tri-state area," "armed and dangerous" and "do not attempt to confront him," were blaring from the TV in the background.

"But first you've got to deal with me. And I haven't decided if you walk out of here at all yet, much less alive. If you call *that* living. So why don't you just sit the hell down and drink your beer and let me think, okay? You got any objection to that plan?"

"Good plan, Charlie. I'll just be over here, then. Drinking my beer." He backed away, rubbing his aching shoulders and lowered himself slowly into the sofa. He kept a close eye on his volatile host the entire time. "Anything good on the tube tonight?"

"You're a damned mental case, you know that? I don't know why I don't just tear you in half, right here. Then I could turn one part over to the police and the other half over to the prince's goons. It's probably the only way I'm going to walk out of this mess with my freaking skull still attached."

Felton kept silent. He knew that Charlie must believe him. Not for old times' sake or anything so romantic, but because it was the only explanation for why the bigger man hadn't torn him limb from limb already. Of course, that wasn't to say he couldn't still change his mind.

"Look, Charlie, you'll be fine. As long as you don't do anything stupid, there's nothing to tie me to this place. Nobody knows I'm here and nobody's going to know. I've just got to get out of town. Tonight. Can you help me? Loan me a bike? Loan, hell—I'll *pay* you for it. Here's the keys to my place. There's a safe beneath the old cast-iron stove. Cash, jewelry, it's all yours. Just give me a bike and a few hundred bucks and you never see me again."

"The bike's not for sale," Charlie said flatly. "What's Plan B?"

"What do you mean it's not for sale? There's at least fifty thousand bucks there," Felton gestured toward where the keys had landed on the floor at Charlie's feet. "You've got five bikes here. Give me your parts-bike for Christsakes."

"I mean they're not for sale. What, are you slow today? That explosion rattle your brains around? Think for a minute. At this point, there may not be anything to tie this mess back to me, but what do you think is going to happen when they stop you at the tunnel—cause you know they're going to have the roadblocks up, right?—and they run a trace on that bike?"

Felton seemed to deflate. "I've got to get out of town," he repeated.

"You're not going anywhere," Charlie said firmly. "You're not even thinking straight at this point. You're all set to go roaring out there and fumble into a police roadblock. And that's only the mortal police! How the heck do you think you're going to make it past what the prince's goons are going to throw up against you? You can't just blow up his right-hand man and think he's going to let you walk away from that. Plus, he's a Nosferatu, which means he's got eyes everywhere and damned near nothing is going to slip past him. Especially not something he's going to want this bad. Hell, you'd be *lucky* if the police got you."

"What am I supposed to do? I can't leave town. I sure as hell can't stay here. I've got a chance if I can get out from under Calebros's reach. I can start over again somewhere else, some other city. New York might be a pretty big pond, but it's still just a pond. The ripples you stir up here aren't likely to follow you very far. I could go to Chicago. Phoenix, maybe. L.A."

"You're not going anywhere tonight. What you need to do is get some rest. We'll talk tomorrow, once you're thinking straight again. I don't want to hear another word out of you until then. You understand me, soldier."

At this, Felton smiled. "Yes, sir."

"I can't hear you, soldier."

"Yes, sir!" Felton barked. "You're a good man, Charlie. I knew you wouldn't let me down."

"Yeah, well I didn't know any such thing, so let's cut the mushy crap and get some sleep. You've got the couch. There's more beer in the fridge, help yourself. And Felton…"

He turned at the sound of his name, startled. Until that moment, he was not aware that Charlie even knew his name. "Yeah, Charlie?"

"Don't stay up all day watching the tube. There's nothing on but talks and soaps and the news. And all of it's phony. And even on the news, nothing ever really happens anymore."

"Good night, Charlie. And thanks."

"Tell you what. If we're both still among the living tomorrow, then you can thank me." He turned to the back bedroom where he was greeted by a chorus of animal sniffings and whimperings. "I said, get down!"

Felton tried not to think about the commotion in the next room and turned back to the TV. Pumping dance music blared from the set. Another one of those damned Cyanight ads everyone was all up in arms about. The scene panned back from the exclusive Manhattan dance club to a panoramic of a gothic

New York skyline. A moment later, sight and sound both dissolved into a burgeoning sickly yellow mushroom cloud.

"New York has just gone virtual," announced the voice over, a James Earl Jones knock-off. "Isn't it time you did too? Cyanight: burning down the Web, one city at a time."

Felton rolled onto his side and pulled his jacket over him like a blanket. Reaching out, he snapped off the TV and let the silence pile high upon him.

Chapter 15
I May Have Hit Her Too Soon

Antigone heard Master Ynnis shout. She felt the concussion of each of the three blows. One…two…three.

Helena sat bolt upright like a child thrown clear of a nightmare. It was all Antigone could do to keep from being thrown herself. She lowered a shoulder and drove her full weight against the adepta in an attempt to fell her. She was only partially successful; the two antagonists crashed to the floor and rolled, Antigone struggling to pin her flailing opponent before the adepta could do one or the other of them lasting harm.

Antigone again heard Master Ynnis's dire warning—that she must wait until the adepta became whole once more, until the Beast was ascendant. Until Helena tried to kill her.

Helena's entire frame shook and buckled—an arcing wave of static blue energy. Suddenly, there was nothing for Antigone hold on to. Her hands, still curled in the grip she'd had upon Helena's shoulders, plunged down and *through* the adepta. There was a resounding crack and a flashfire of pain. Antigone jerked back a wrist that was bent at an unsettling angle.

She rolled, cradling the broken wrist to her chest. She knew she had only a moment's respite, if that long. She set her teeth and pulled. More cracking of bone, this time falling back into its accustomed place. The wave of pain washed over her, bringing with it the first circling of the black gulls.

Waiting was no longer an option.

The lines of Helena's face wavered and then snapped back into focus. Antigone hit her with everything she had, her good fist smashing into the adepta's jaw. It was a blow that would have broken the neck of a heavyweight.

Helena crumpled back to the floor in a shower of crackling blue arcane energy, her signal weakening, breaking up.

"I'm losing her!" Antigone shouted at the com port. "I...I may have hit her too soon. What do we do now?"

There was no response.

"Ynnis, can you hear me?"

Silence.

"Status of communications node?" she called angrily.

"Connection to regent's sanctum open and operational."

"Location of Ynnis, Master?"

"Ynnis, Master, is located in the regent's sanctum."

"Then why the hell doesn't he answer? Never mind, don't answer that." She turned her full attention back to Helena. It was clear the adepta was fading fast.

"Damn it, you're not going to die on me!" she shouted directly into Helena's face. She bunched a fist in the front of Helena's robes and tried to shake her, but she could get no grip on the shifting material.

"We need you! This chantry needs you. Sturbridge needs you. Get up!" She rained a series of sharp slaps down on both sides of the adepta's face, forehand and back. Some of them landed, some did not, but Antigone was far past caring about such trifles.

At the mention of Sturbridge's name, Helena's eyes flickered open briefly. But there was no hint of consciousness behind the eyelids, only the unbroken whites overlaid with spiderwebs of black lines clustered in the corners—the afterimage of dried-out, disused veins.

"Helena. Listen to me. We need you back here and we need you now. Why aren't you at your post?" She was rewarded for her rebuke with a crackle of static that ran the entire length of the adepta's body.

"We've got one hell of a systems integrity failure here and you're the only one who can shut the damned thing down before we have a full network meltdown!" No response.

"We've got a guardian spirit gone renegade in the novice *domicilium*. It's burning the place to the ground. There are three novices trapped inside!" Nothing.

"Damn it, I need you to get me into the regent's sanctum! Sturbridge is inside, but she's not responding. She may be hurt or dead, I don't know. Master Ynnis went in after her, but now he's not answering either. He said something about..."

Helena's eyes flew open. Her hands shot out. The unexpected lunge would have knocked Antigone over backward, had the adepta's arms had any more substance to them. As it was, Antigone felt only the slightest shudder as the open palms contacted her robes and pressed onward until they had sunk to the elbow within her body.

She squirmed, fighting down a scream. Her first instinct was to free herself before the limbs impaling her took on a greater solidity. But she badly misjudged the intent of the attack.

As Antigone twisted, Helena's questing hand found the object of its blind groping. With a blow as patient and precise as that of a jeweler's hammer, she reached out her index finger and tapped once, gently, upon Antigone's heart.

Antigone was rooted to the spot. She tried to move, but her limbs were numb and heavy. They would not answer her urgent commands. She tried to speak, but her mouth would not form words, her lungs would not draw air. There was a weight in the pit of her stomach—a surety which churned and curled in upon itself. Any moment now it would emerge from its larval dread into a full-fledged panic. The novice's startled eyes met those of the adept. In them, Antigone expected to see her final death descending upon her in a flurry of black wings. What she found instead startled her, shook her.

Within the eyes of the adepta, Antigone could find no reflection of herself at all. Helena's thoughts had already turned from her, returning to her one, all-consuming struggle. Antigone no longer played into the calculation at all. She had become suddenly beside the point.

Anger and indignation rose within her. But the adepta did not flinch away from the fire in her stare. Instead, she held their gazes locked. The pupils of the adepta's eyes widened, seeming to beckon, to draw her inward. Antigone wavered uncertainly on the brink of that dark aperture. Peering over the edge, she caught a momentary glimpse of the struggle raging within—a struggle not against her, but against the rising Beast that gnashed at its fraying tether. Gazing full upon the face of the Beast—a canine form wrought from purest shadow, its oversized jaws gnashing like those of a mastiff—Antigone knew with certainty that it was a fight that Helena could not hope to win. She was far too weak to hold the ravaging Beast in check much longer.

But in that moment of clarity, at the meeting of the three pairs of eyes, Antigone realized something. It was only the adepta's weakness that had kept the Beast at bay so long. Like her own clumsy efforts to pin Helena down, the surging of the Beast could find no handle upon her fluid shiftings. Antigone now knew with certainty that it was not Helena's body alone which had fallen into schism, it was her entire identity. Through her miscarried and forbidden rite, she had become a divided self.

But the Beast was about to change all that, to knock down the walls, to bring things back into sharp focus. Back to the primal, the undeniable. It was a magic as old as time. The spilling of blood.

Antigone could only watch helplessly as Helena turned and walked purposefully toward the diagram. Without a backward glance, the adepta crossed over and vanished from view.

The intercom crackled and a voice, nearly lost beneath a roar of flames, was shouting, "It's no good. We can't get to them. They're trapped on the far side. The room won't depressurize properly, so we're trying to do this the old fashioned way — firebreaks and bucket brigades. The breaks are holding for the moment, but the wardings that form the backbone had to be thrown together pretty hastily. They're taking a beating and there's no telling how long they're going to be able to contain the blaze. I don't even want to think about what happens if that thing in there takes it into its head to go for a little stroll. Without clearing the systems failure and rebooting, we're not going to be able to depressurize the adjoining corridors either. That means we've got no real way of containing this thing. We may be looking at an evacuation scenario here. Do you read? Repeat: possible evacuation scenario."

Antigone wanted to answer him, to shout at him. But an icy certainty had taken hold of her, spreading out from the exact point where Helena had tapped upon her heart. She was powerless under the weight of that conviction, unable to move or speak. An eternity of helplessness stretched before her. How long would it be, she wondered, before someone wandered in here and found her like this, rooted to the spot? It might be quite some time. If plans for an evacuation were already underway, it was quite possible that the spreading flames would reach her long before her comrades thought it safe to return to the chantry.

She again felt the tentative caress of dark wings, but she could not rouse herself even to bat them away. Soon they were all around her, the black carrion birds, those harbingers of death. They strutted and cocked their heads, looking at her askance. The boldest among them pecked experimentally at the hem of her robes. She suffered all their presumption in silence.

Emboldened by her inaction, the murder of crows pressed her all the more closely. She felt the first sharp prick of beak tearing free a strip of cool dead flesh. It tossed its head and the pale, black-veined morsel vanished down its gullet. A second bird drew in close and another gobbet of flesh was torn away. She could not bring herself to resist them. They were well within their rights. She willed her eyes to close, but it was not her eyelids, but rather dark feathers that descended over her sight.

The sound of footfalls called her back to herself. Heavy footfalls. Someone struggling under a burden. She willed her eyes to open again, but the smothering wings seemed unwilling to oblige her a second time.

She could not gauge how much time had passed. Nights? Years? She felt light and buoyant as if her bones, so long confined within the prison of the flesh, were finally laid bare and free to walk about on their own. Picked clean.

Peeking through the delicate fan of black feathers, she saw Helena emerge from the diagram. In her arms she bore the unmoving body of Master Ynnis. She carried him to the nearest sofa and laid him out there, respectfully and precisely. He looked like a corpse.

That was silly, Antigone thought, feeling the first caress of rising hysteria. He *was* a corpse. They were all corpses. She meant that he looked like a new corpse. One that hadn't been properly broken in yet. One that had not yet gotten his land legs back after the long journey by skiff.

She kept expecting him, willing him, to get up. To push himself up off the sofa and mutter something enigmatic with his usual self-deprecating smile—to apologize for being late.

Yes, that was precisely the tenor of his humor. You could kill him and he would apologize for being "late."

Master Ynnis showed no inclination toward rising or helping her. She looked to Helena, but then glanced away again hastily. Antigone had no idea how the adepta had managed to keep the Beast at bay so long. You could see it overflowing its channel and consuming her. Even from a distance, Antigone could make out that the hair of Helena's arms had grown dark and coarse. Her mouth would not quite close any longer around the wet, oversized canines. Her entire form was hunched, as if curling inward into a compact ball of rippling muscle. Crouching to pounce.

Chapter 16
Urinating on a Bonfire

Felton was already awake when Charlie got up. He hadn't slept much. About three in the afternoon, he had given up entirely and flipped on the tube. There was nothing on, of course. Nothing but rehashes of the bombing. Not exactly what he needed to see right now. But he let it run, forced himself to watch.

Fortunately, most of the blast had expanded outward from the observation deck, and none of the residual fires had really taken hold. You just couldn't fight a fire a hundred stories in the air. Not by any conventional means. The pressure from a street hydrant, even boosted by a pumper truck, couldn't force the water up that high.

They had done a few fly-overs dropping flame-retardant chemicals, and there was an interview with one of the pilots they had rushed in from fighting forest fires in Nevada or someplace. He was photogenic and self-deprecating. The gist of the sound bite was that they had been lucky. He was just saying something colorful about urinating on a bonfire when the interviewer cut to the next segment.

There were the mandatory bits of poking microphones into the faces of "eye-witnesses," none of whom Felton had noticed anywhere near the scene. He imagined that these were the people of the aftermath—that inevitable crowd of gawkers who, alerted by the noise of the explosion, had swarmed to the scene. Someone reported seeing a man fleeing the building. A man he described as "a whacko survivalist type. Mid-thirtiesish, bald, kind of paunchy. And running for his life."

Not a very flattering description, perhaps, but more accurate than Felton would have expected. The typical witness reports seldom produced anything more concrete than "It was a guy, a white guy. And he was waving these guns around and shooting up the place."

The picture cut to the grainy close-up from the black-and-white security camera. Felton rolled his eyes and his twin on the sofa mirrored the gesture. It had to be the twentieth time he'd seen the shot. He kept thinking it would get less embarrassing over time, but so far he was disappointed.

The scene cut back to the anchor desk and a newsreader who obviously had not been up all night. "In a related story, internet giant Cyanight Entertainment has pulled the latest in its series of controversial ads. Cyanight spokesman Adam Graves told a press conference earlier today that it would be 'insensitive' to continue to run the ad—which shows the destruction of New York City in a nuclear explosion—in light of current events. Graves denied that advertisements with strong violent content encouraged actual violence. 'These ads no more promote acts of violence and terrorism than watching old documentary newsreels promotes war. I don't want to make light of this event. This bombing is a great tragedy. It is a miracle that more people were not hurt or killed, and our deepest sympathies go out to those families who are suffering.'"

A beercan popped just behind him and Felton started. Charlie was leaning over the back of the sofa. "You been to sleep yet?"

Felton nodded and took the beer without enthusiasm. "Thanks. A little. I've just been up a couple of hours. I keep thinking they might show something. Something useful, I mean."

Charlie took a long gulp of beer. "I've been thinking about what you said last night. About being set up. About getting out of town."

"And?"

"And I don't know. It seems like too much of a coincidence. You showing up to make a hit at the same time somebody decides to blow up the Empire State Building. You in trouble, Felton? Some other trouble, I mean. Is there somebody who would want you dead?"

"Hell, I don't know, Charlie! I've been going over and over it in my mind. But it just won't click. Who'd want me dead? Sure, some Sabbat bastards; we've been fighting them for years. But all that's over now, isn't it? I mean, we won, right? So what gives?"

Charlie shook his head. "No, you're right. That doesn't make any sense. For one, it's not the Sabbat's style. If they wanted you...well, they've had plenty of shots, haven't they? And some pretty good ones, too." He punched Felton in the shoulder, ungently. "Hey, you remember that time we stumbled into that clutch of them holed up in this sort of burial mound thingie down by the river?"

"Well, those guys sure aren't likely to be holding a grudge." Felton replied, smiling for the first time this evening. "They kicked our ass up one side and down the other. I didn't think we were going to be able to drag your sorry carcass out of there. There was a point where, if they would have just asked nice, I would have run out and brought them back some barbecue sauce so that they could spit-roast the rest of you bastards."

Charlie said, "Well, that's what I mean. The Sabbat, or at least the war-packs that have been sniffing around this place for the last few years, they're just not that subtle. They're cocky. They're arrogant. And they're used to getting what they want.

If the Sabbat had wanted you out of the way—even after their fall from power—they would have kicked down your door and dragged you out."

"Give me a little credit," Felton said. "I've spent at least as much time covering my tracks against just such an unwelcome house call as I've spent busting in other folks' front doors."

"But if they knew you would be at the Empire State Building, they would have jumped you there, not blown up the building and tried to frame you. And they would have taken you, too. I can't believe you went on a high-profile hit like that without any backup."

"Backup wasn't in the briefing," Felton said.

"Neither was the building blowing up," Charlie replied. "I'm liking this briefing less and less every time we talk about it. Can I see it again?"

Felton scooped up the rolled and wrinkled manila envelope off the floor. "Help yourself. If I never see the damned thing again it will be too soon."

Charlie was flipping pages. "And you're sure this is legit. This handwriting the same as you remember from previous missions? There's no way the dossier could have been tampered with? When we were all inside the meeting maybe?"

Felton just shook his head. "I don't know. I don't think so." He sat in silence for a long while. When he did answer, it was clear his thoughts had not been on Charlie's question. "You ever miss it?" he asked.

Charlie laughed uncomfortably and then grew quiet. "Fighting with the Sabbat, you mean? Nah, I don't miss them. And I sure don't miss getting shot at or run over or clawed up. Man, I hated those bastards. Really hated them, I mean. With one of those hurt-'em-on-sight kinds of hate. You know what I mean. The kind of hate where your eyes film over with blood and it's like you're watching yourself over your own shoulder. Like you're in a late-night movie or something. Not acting or anything stupid like that. Just watching yourself on TV. But all that's changed now. We won, right?" He slapped Felton heartily on the back. "Yes sir, we won."

"But would you—I mean, if you could—would you go back?"

Charlie covered up the long pause by throwing down the rest of his beer. Then he gave an exaggerated salute, crushing the can against his forehead. "Dead soldier," he said. "You need another?"

"I'm fine, thanks. I try to keep it to just one before breakfast," Felton added.

"Suit yourself. If I were in your shoes, though, it would take a six-pack to get me to the point where I would even think about braving that front door." He returned with two beers and handed one to Felton despite his objections. "You really miss it?"

"At least with the Sabbat, you knew what you were up against." Felton considered. "You knew who would waste you as soon as look at you. And you knew who was on your team. And damn it, that was important. It meant something. Now, everything is all cloak and dagger. Behind closed doors. Solo missions. You might laugh, but you know, it just about killed me when we broke up the old squads. Watching all the guys, everybody we'd fought alongside of all those years, just kind of drift off like that. It killed me. I kept thinking, wait a minute, we won! Where the hell is everyone going? We won. But all of a sudden, it was like there was no more Sabbat so there was no reason to stay. And it only got worse the more you thought about it. Before long it was like everything we had fought for just didn't matter anymore."

"You having second thoughts, hero?" Charlie's face was solemn, with no hint of mocking in his voice.

"Yeah, some hero. One who doesn't have sense enough to know when to quit fighting. The bullets stopped flying a month ago. So how come I'm still throwing punches? How come I'm still out doing raids and hits, the whole works? I'll tell you something Charlie, it was ten times better when we were fighting the Sabbat. Because at least then I knew we were right. I knew they were hits and not murders. Now? Now I'm not so sure."

"The war's changed, man. That's all. You know how we used to fight it. And you were good at it. Damn good. You've got nothing to be ashamed of. But there's a new war on now. And it's being fought every night in the streets, just like the old one. Only everything's turned all upside-down. You ever watch westerns, Felton? On late-night TV?"

"Sure, some," Felton admitted grudgingly.

"Well, it's like a western. Now, in these westerns there was this place and they called it Dodge City—I guess because there wasn't a damn thing you could do to prevent the place from taking a poke at you; the most you could do was dodge and hope for the best. It was that kind of place. There wasn't any law in Dodge. Well, none to speak of. The sheriff, maybe he was scared or maybe he was on the take—because that was the best way to cover up being scared—to arrange things so that it wasn't in your interest to stand up for anything...."

"Or maybe he just didn't care," Felton saw where his host was going and warmed to the topic. "Maybe he'd rather splash through his sewers and diddle with his rats than lift a finger to keep folks from killing one another in the streets."

"I don't think they had sewers," Charlie said. "Rats I'll grant you. But never mind. Look, the point is it was a different kind of war there, in Dodge. Not the kind folks were used to. Sure there were old veterans there, folks who had fought on either side in the War of Northern Aggression—"

"Um, I think they call it the 'Civil War' around here," Felton interrupted.

"And I imagine there are some that would call a hand grenade a handshake, but that's really no business of mine. What I was trying to say was that these old timers, no matter how good infantrymen or cavalrymen or artillerists they might have been, they didn't just show up understanding the new ways—the swagger, the saloon, the showdown. It was a whole new war. Sure, some of them caught on, but most never did. Boot Hill was filled with little wooden crosses for all those who just never caught on."

"And what if I don't want to fight a new war?" Felton challenged. "I was fine with the old war. I wasn't any fonder of the Sabbat than you were, Charlie. But I was good at it. I'm still here—we're both still here—and they're not. That should mean something."

"Yeah, it means it's you instead of some Tzimisce shovel-head moping around and getting all nostalgic about the good old days. That war is over, man. You've got to roll with it or, I'm telling you, you're going to get blindsided. You're not only going to end up a victim, buddy, you're going to wind up being one of the first men out."

"I've already gotten myself blindsided," Felton replied flatly. "We've been through some tough scrapes before, but I don't know how the heck I'm supposed to get out of this one. I've just got no clue."

"That's exactly what I've been trying to tell you. The old ways of problem solving just don't apply anymore. The days when balls and an extra clip of ammo added up to a fighting chance, they're over."

"Just like that? I don't get any say in the matter. It's just over? Damn it, I fought that war for over ten years! I lost…shit, I'm not even going to go into what I've lost. But a lot of good men gave their lives so that New York would not become just another Sabbat playground."

"A lot of folks," Charlie replied, "had the good sense not to get up again after they were shot dead the first time."

"Damn it, that's not what I'm talking about and you know it." His raised voice was greeted with a warning growl from the back room. It brought him up short. "I don't know. I just don't know anymore. What the hell am I supposed to do?"

Charlie had no good answer to give him. They sat in silence, Felton trying to tune out the news, Charlie flipping idly through the dossier, as if hoping some vital clue would just drop out into his lap. As if it were stuck between two pages and by repeatedly thumbing through he would eventually jog it loose. "I wish I knew if this briefing were legit. If we only knew that, we'd know whether or not we could go to back to the Conventicle and get some help with all—"

"No. Absolutely not." Felton was grim. "There's just no way I can risk going back. Even if somebody did pull a switch with the folders, that somebody would have to have known an awful lot about our operation—how we worked, when and where we met. No. I can't chance it. I don't know who set me up, but whoever it was, I'm sure not putting myself back within his reach again so he can take another shot at me. Maybe put me out of commission for good this time."

"Settle down. I'm just trying to think through this, okay? I know this whole situation looks real bad from where you're sitting. But I'm on your side, all right? This mess doesn't just smell fishy, it stinks to high heaven. It's just too much of a coincidence that you get the nod for a hit that's to go down in the exact same time and place that the whole damn building is blown up. But what I don't understand is why. You think someone was trying to kill *you*?"

"Hell, Charlie, I told you I don't know. Were going around in circles here." Seeing the look on his host's face, Felton forced himself to calm down and think. "No. Of course not. Nobody's going to blow up the damned Empire State Building just to try to kill me. But if someone knew that the deal was going down, they might take advantage of the opportunity to set me up—to make sure I would be in the wrong place at the wrong time."

Charlie shook his head. "I still don't see how anybody could have singled you out to take the fall. I mean, it was all the luck of the dice. Any one of us could have drawn out the dragon. Even the Bonespeaker couldn't have known who would pull the 'black spot.'"

Felton would not meet his eye. "Yeah, well. He couldn't have known. I'll grant you that."

"What are you saying? I've known you too long not to know when you're holding something back. You need to come clean with me right now or I'm putting your sorry butt back out on the curb. So what is it? Was there some kind of fix in on this draw?"

"No, nothing like that," Felton said.

"So what is it? Are you trying to tell me that this whole Rite of Drawing Down the Dragon thing is rigged? Why would you even bother going through the motions if you knew the game was crooked? Damn it, I'm trying to help you and you're still playing me. Well, I'm tired of being played. So tell me what the hell is going on or get the hell out of here."

Felton rose quickly, as if expecting things to come to blows. "Nobody's playing you, Charlie. I'm the one being set up here, remember? If the draw is rigged, it's news to me. I don't know how they'd pull something like that off anyway. You mean some kind of sleight of hand?"

"Why the hell not sleight of hand? All the Bonespeaker would need is two bags—one that's all dragons and one that's nothing but winds. Hell, it wouldn't even have to be the Speaker. Anybody could slip a few extra dragons into the bag when it was his turn. That would be enough to stack the deck pretty heavily against the guy sitting next to him."

"Nobody stacked the deck against me. Nobody switched the bags," Felton admitted.

"Then what the hell are you getting at?"

There was a long pause. "Look, Charlie. I didn't draw the dragon. That's all."

"What the hell do you mean, you didn't draw the dragon? I was there, remember? You said, 'Soap...' Charlie trailed off. "You sorry son of a bitch. It wasn't the dragon!"

"South wind," Felton shrugged.

"Why'd you do it, man? Did the Speaker put you up to it? I heard the two of you talking, but I couldn't make out what you were saying. Did he threaten you?"

"No, nothing like that. He was goading me, trying to get under my skin. But that wasn't it. It was just...oh, hell Charlie, you know how it is. I was bored and fed up with all this cloak and dagger and just spoiling for an honest, knock-down drag-out fight. A little bit of action. You know, just like old times..."

"So you lied. You know, this is likely to go down as the dumbest thing you ever did. Not that you haven't done some really stupid things before. But if this one doesn't kill you—kill the both of us, for that matter—it's not because you didn't deserve it."

"Thanks, Charlie. I knew you'd understand."

"Shut up. I'm not sure if I'm still talking to you. No, wait, I am. Somebody's got to tell you what a dumbass you are. Nobody set you up, Felton. You set *yourself* up. You didn't need any help. You went right ahead and stuck your own neck in the noose. And now you're going to go ahead and pull the lever for them too and drop the trap door out from under you. You think you're going to be able to waltz out of town, just like that?"

"You got a better plan? I can't just sit around here and wait for them to kick down your front door. Not that I don't appreciate your trying to help me out, but I've got to *do* something, Charlie. The more we sit here thinking about it, the more we're going to snipe at one another. And the less likely that either one of us is going to walk out of here."

"All right. So let's say the first thing we need to do is to find somewhere for you to lay low for a while. Somewhere safe. There's always the possibility that somebody from the Conventicle will try to make contact with me here, and that would be bad news for both of us. Lord knows I don't advertise my whereabouts, but you managed to find this place. And if you could, that means somebody else could too."

"What do you have in mind?" Felton replied cautiously.

"Is there anybody else you can count on to—" Charlie began and then broke off. "Never mind. Stupid question. If there were you wouldn't be here, right?"

Felton nodded slowly. "I guess some of the guys are still around. The ones that drifted off after we beat the Sabbat. After we broke up the squads. But after this…I don't know, Charlie. My face has been all over the news. I just don't know if I can count on their goodwill anymore. Sure, in the old days it was different. I would have taken a bullet for any of those guys and I'd be willing to bet they'd do the same for me. But now? What am I to them now? Nothing, that's what. Or worse than nothing, a liability. An old war buddy who didn't have sense enough to quit fighting once the war was over. They've got other things going on now, other angles. They don't need me coming around and messing things up for them."

"Yeah, I know how that goes."

"Aw, come on, Charlie. It's different with you. I don't mean to sound ungrateful, but you're still in the game. You may be fed up with it, but you're still a part of it."

"I'm a part of it all right. A part that should just sell your sorry hindparts to the highest bidder—get what price I can for you and count myself lucky."

"That was a risk I knew I was running when I came here. I'm glad to know that I can count on you, Charlie."

"Don't be too sure. You get to be too much of a pain in my butt and I'm going to cut my losses. Now shut up and let me think. We need to find someplace for you to lie low. You've got to go underground for a while."

"Oh, no. Not underground. The last thing I need right now is to go playing into the hands of the damned Nossies…"

"Relax," Charlie interrupted. "You're so freaking literal. I didn't mean *underground* underground. Steering clear of the Nossies is probably reason enough not to go back to the Conventicle right now. Did you see all the new faces at the last gathering? Everybody was talking about some big 'defection' a few nights ago. From what I could piece together it sounded like at least two or three of those newcomers had just bailed on the prince and come over to our side."

Felton whistled. "Still too risky."

"Yeah, you said it. With the defectors, that would bring the Nossie contingent up to five or six members. They might even be in the majority now. And despite their break with the prince, I wouldn't want to have to bet my safety on every single one of them being really grateful to you for just going ahead and blowing up his right-hand man. It sets a bad precedent."

"But I didn't blow him up!" Felton objected.

"And you think your story about what you were really doing there is going to win you many fans among that crowd? They tend to be a little overprotective of their own. Even if we were to say that none of the newcomers is a plant—a long shot at best—are you willing to bet your miserable unlife that all of them have burned their bridges already? Emmett was one of their own. And these guys might not have any beef against him at all."

"Well, I'm sure as hell not going back there. We've already established that," Felton said.

"Fine. But what I'm trying to say is that, if that's the reception you can expect from the Nossies that have joined our side, think what kind of welcome the ones who have remained loyal to their prince are planning for you. I imagine they are out, even as we speak, scouring the city. They've probably got a few 'pointed' questions they'd like to put to you."

"I'm not arguing with you. I can't leave town, can't stay here, can't look up any old buddies, can't go back to the Conventicle, can't go underground. So where does that leave us?"

Charlie considered. "I've got a friend I want you to meet." He raised a hand to forestall Felton's objections. "If I didn't think we could count on her, I sure as hell wouldn't put my neck on the line to take you there."

Felton swallowed his initial retort. "Her?"

"Yeah, her. You got a problem with that? Don't tell me you're not interested in girls anymore."

"Great. Just what I need. A freaking matchmaker. Where do you know this 'friend' from?"

"Trading," Charlie replied. "Bikes and guns. Which reminds me, I saw you were still toting around that foreign crap when you came in. We'll swap those out. We're upgrading your image."

"Great," Felton repeated without enthusiasm. "Six-guns, I imagine."

Charlie slapped him on the back. "Come on, let's find you a bike."

"But you told me that you wouldn't—"

"You're right," Charlie interrupted. "I wouldn't. Give you one of my bikes so you could ride off like an idiot and get both you and my stuff shot up? Yeah, that's a great idea. But we've got somebody to meet and you sure as hell ain't riding up behind me."

"What's wrong with this one right here?" Felton challenged, indicating the monstrous bike that dominated the room.

"Nothing's wrong with it; it's what's wrong with you. You're not half man enough to take that bike out. And it ain't even finished yet. By the time it's done you're not going to be able to pull yourself up even to the kickstart. That's the kind of bike that makes folks small or makes them legends."

Felton snorted. "Yeah, right. You're not fooling anybody, you know. You can't even get it out the door anymore, can you? Well, can you?" he called after the retreating figure.

Charlie was already halfway down the steps. He didn't even turn.

Chapter 17
Bones Never Meant to Run In

*D*amn it, that wasn't supposed to happen, Antigone thought angrily. Master Ynnis said that Helena would be too far gone in the clutches of the Beast to pull off any kind of thaumaturgic effect—much less something as severe as reaching right inside her and paralyzing her with a single touch.

Antigone was not certain why she had not already slipped into the deep, healing torpor. She was not sure how she managed to even stand, although she suspected the paralysis was largely to blame for that as well.

Somehow she had to stop Helena. Stop her before she killed someone—Master Ynnis, Regent Sturbridge, maybe even Antigone herself. She was not afraid for her own life. Not at any fundamental level. But even inactivity now would be closely akin to murder. The emergency response team was sorely pressed holding the rogue spirit at bay in the novice *domicilium*. Without Helena's security codes, they would not be able to contain it for long. The fires would spread, the chantry would have to be evacuated, and many would perish in the flames.

Since all her voluntary muscles seemed to have failed her, Antigone reached out with the only tools at her disposal. She plunged deep within herself, trying, through sheer force of will, to melt the icy grip on her heart.

But she found even that way barred to her. A shadowy figure loomed over her, vast and forbidding. Its face was elongated and almost canine. It smiled down upon her benignly, but blocked her way forward with crossed crook and flail. She threw herself against him, this silent warden of the dead, but he was unmoved by her furious onslaught.

Antigone pummeled his chest with both fists, but the ceremonial breastplate of woven reed cut her hands as if it were made of sand and stone. She threw herself against him again and again, trying to daze him with a flurry of stunning blows. She tried to pitch him off balance, to slip past. She launched vicious bone-snapping strikes at his knees and ankles. But it was all to no avail. Even where her punches landed upon the most vulnerable flesh of neck, kidney and groin, it was like striking cool ebon marble.

Frustrated, she fell back panting and defeated. "You have no right to keep me out!" she raged at the brooding Jackal God. "People will die if I do not—" she broke off in the face of his sardonic smile, slow realization washing over her. What did it matter to the Keeper of the Dead if a few more lives were lost— especially when those deaths were long overdue?

"No. I won't let you," she raged. "I have paid your bloodprice. Many times over."

If the dark one were impressed, he kept his stoic peace.

"Why don't you answer me? I said answer!"

"*So impatient, little one.*" The voice was little more than a whisper, but it swelled to fill the torchlit corridor. The gentle tone was so far removed from what she expected of the barking Jackal God that at first she failed to realize that it had spoken. Certainly no hint of movement from the chiseled features betrayed the fact. She was about to repeat her bellowed demand when she became aware of the murmurings. They seemed to arise from a low buzzing, a vibration transmitted directly by way of the unlikely medium of the bones of her skull.

"You are fiercely proud of your death, little one. That is well. But you will not heed it. How will you hear the answer when it comes, if your head is full of only shouting and striking?"

Antigone fell back as if struck, stammering, uncertain. "What is this? What is this place? Let me go. I've…I've got to go back. I've got to stop Helena."

"Always running. It is no wonder you never get anywhere. Walk with me."

It was not a request. Antigone jerked forward mechanically, but immediately felt that something was wrong. That this was not at all what was expected of her.

"I…I don't know how," she admitted.

There was a low chuckle. It began as a tingling where her skull met her spine and quickly spread to cover her entire scalp. Her ears rang, straining to catch the sound that was simply not available to them. "Better," her skull whispered to her. "You are remembering. If you would walk with me, you must step out of your skin and dance in your bones. Here, take my hand."

Antigone felt more than slightly ridiculous. The carved statue before her did not move, much less extend a hand to help her. Nonetheless, she reached out, stretching trustingly, like a child. She felt a reassuring pressure on her hand, although she could see that there was nothing there. It squeezed once, almost playfully, and then gave a sharp tug.

A cold panic broke over her as she saw the first hint of gleaming white bone tear outward through her fingertips. She screamed, watching knucklebones emerge from the parting flesh. She felt a rending pain all along the front of her body — the tops of her feet, her shins, thighs, abdomen, breasts, face. Every surface burned as if her entire body were being crushed beneath a great weight. The pain swelled until she thought she could take it no longer, that she would surely black out.

And then something gave way. Some unconscious barrier of her own making, rather than a tangible obstacle external to her. There was a swift rush of disorientation and a sharp crack that she felt in the hollow of her neck. Then she was stepping forward, sloughing off the heavy, unmanageable garment of flesh and sinew. She stretched luxuriantly, cracking her knuckles high above her head. She rippled, bones snapping the entire length of her body. A great breathless sigh. She felt unspeakably free.

She could not remain still. She poured out her freedom through the only means of expression at her disposal. She bounded, she plummeted, she danced.

Only gradually did she become aware of the presence of the other. Her outpouring of emotion had been spontaneous, without any shred of concern for communication, much less an audience. It brought her up short.

Slowly, she turned to face the Laughing God. She could not see him; he wore no visible form, not even his bones. But perhaps they had turned to dust centuries ago. Still, she knew unerringly where he was. He was a presence. An inhuman force. Like gravity or tempest. Her bones reoriented, drawn to him, falling inward.

The other laughed again and she felt its warmth hum along the conduit of her bones. She pivoted, an antenna tuned to that low, roiling laugh. "Come here, little one. These bones were never meant to run in. You must learn to be still. But I am pleased that you had the opportunity to dance once. Now come here and let us see what you shall be."

She drew closer and felt his hands encircle her like quilted comforters drawn up over her head. She surrendered to the warmth of that caress. The blankets pressed down upon her until she thought that she would smother. They rolled her between them, poking and prodding her into a tiny ball. Then she felt herself taken by either arm and tugged. She did not know which way to turn. The pull became painful and she cried out, but it was not a human voice that emerged, but the sharp cry of a predatory bird.

Her arms were stretched impossibly thin. She felt she could barely hold them up. Then suddenly the force that had been supporting them was withdrawn and her arms flapped clumsily under their own unfamiliar weight.

She felt cold, alone, exposed. She shivered, a hollow rattling of bone racing the entire length of her gawky body. She stumbled forward, more hopping than walking as she tried to catch her balance. Everything was out of kilter. She could not seem to get her feet under her.

Then suddenly she was falling. She flailed wildly, hearing the wind whistle through each of her hollow bones. It was a mournful sound. A wailing of sea cliff losing, inch by inch, the slow battle to the pounding surf.

"Always in such a hurry," the rushing wind seemed to say. Although, she realized, it was not the wind that was rushing. "Here, you'll catch your death of cold."

Something dark and heavy wrapped around her. It looked alarmingly like the flayed hide of a jackal. The hollowed-out face that formed the hood kept flapping maddeningly against the back of her head as she plummeted. She pulled the skin more tightly about her in hopes that it would block out the worst of the biting cold, only to discover it was not fur under her hands, but black feathers. In surprise, she lost her grip on the garment. Instead of being whipped away by the winds, however, she found it was still stuck fast to her, fused to the framework of bones. It burned with a searing heat and she screamed again.

But the sound that emerged was not her voice, but the familiar low, rumbling laugh. "My little one. My precious little hawk. It is time to see whether or not you will take to your new wings. But return to me soon."

But I...I don't know how to return. I don't know how I came to be here.

"That is no great mystery. You stopped running. Nothing more. When you have done what is needful, you will stop again—if you can remember the trick. And then you will return to me here. I have a riddle for you still, and a gift, so you must take pains to find your way back to me. I know you will, in the end. They all do. But take care not to hurry. You will promise me that, won't you? My dear little one. That you will not hurry? There is nothing quite so silly as a little bird trying to run."

Antigone strained to pull out of the dive. She could feel the ground rushing up at her.

Helena stopped cold at the edge of the circle of apportation. It was the sound of Antigone's cry that brought her up short. It cut cleanly through the low-lying mists that shrouded Helena's awareness—the exhalations of the grave that always proceeded from the maw of the Beast. It was one of its most baleful powers. Unleashed, the mists went before the Beast to disorient its prey, to drive it to desperation and despair. Some distant part of Helena's mind, wandering the twisting tracks of that fog-bound forestscape, recognized Antigone's call and turned instinctively toward it.

There was no way the novice should have been able to mutter a sound, much less slump to the floor—which was exactly what she did next. Helena took a step toward Antigone as if to catch her.

But the novice did not just collapse; rather, she seemed to collapse *inward*. With its supporting framework suddenly jerked out from beneath it, her robe sloughed to the floor.

"No!" Appalled, Helena lashed out through the fog, clutching at the robes. The blow she had struck the novice should not have killed her, much less reduced her instantly to dust and ashes. It could not be.

To her relief, something still stirred there, within the voluminous folds of fabric. Something desperately flailing, beating, struggling to rise again.

Helena snapped the edge of the robe sharply, like shaking out a sheet. A hawk broke from the garment as she staggered back. It was the black of a mineshaft in hue, save for a diamond-shaped patch of frost on its breast. It fluttered wildly, fighting for altitude. Righting itself, it wasted no time in swooping immediately down upon the adept.

Still clutching the hem of the empty robe, Helena threw her hands protectively up before her face, shielding her eyes from cruel beak and talon. She could feel the hot tracks of blood streaking her face. She tasted the salt tang of it trickling past the corner of her mouth.

Helena was too startled by this sudden transformation to properly muster her defenses. Antigone had never before shown any great aptitude for the magical arts. Her attempts to work the mastery of the blood had always ended in only frustration. It was a continual source of embarrassment for the young neophyte.

To pull off a major transmutation suddenly was almost unthinkable.

Helena batted at the swooping bird. *Have to think. Have to stay calm.* She was still terribly weak from the miscarried rite. She was acutely aware that she was trapped between the two ravening beasts—the hawk that clawed at her face and the darker, more personal nemesis that tore at her innards, trying to rend its way out. The Beast had fought its way very close to the surface. She could feel its coarse black fur bristling on her forearms, feel the press of its long canine fangs forcing her jaws open. She must be especially vigilant now. She could not allow either adversary to get the advantage of her.

It was their very hunger, she knew, that was their weakness. Their desperate thrashing, clawing, swooping, pouncing, tumbling. Always in motion, always running.

The hawk could not hope to hover motionless in the air. It had to keep moving or fall. On the high thermals, perhaps, it could steal a trick from the river's book, to be always moving, never changing. Gliding forward while itself remaining perfectly motionless.

But here, here in this enclosed space, a hawk could be nothing but frantic.

The other beast, the carrion-eater that gnawed upon her rotting carcass from within, it too was trapped. Restlessly pacing off the confines of its fleshly cell. Racing up and down, hurling itself bodily against the walls of its prison.

Confinement only fed their desperation.

Helena knew, only too well, how dangerous a cornered animal could be. She had trapped Antigone once already, imprisoned her within the paralyzed husk of her own decaying body. But she had not counted upon the strength of the novice's desperation. Somehow Antigone had found the strength to burst from that prison. Helena only hoped that in so doing, Antigone had not destroyed the shell of her human form altogether. That was always the greatest risk in transformations—that the potent magics would utterly consume the original form of the thaumaturge.

Whatever the truth of the matter, Helena needed to bring this bird back to ground.

Whirling Antigone's discarded robe like a net, she entangled the screaming avian. She drew the loose ends of the fabric tightly against her chest—trying to smother the attacks by pinning its wings. The hawk struggled furiously, buffeting against her, its beak still striking true through the fabric.

But now Helena, although herself weary and unsteady on her feet, had the upper hand. The crumpled wad of fabric drew tighter, assuming the recognizable form of the bird trapped within. Still Helena drew the cloth tighter, until she could see the clearly defined outline of the bird's head.

With one swift motion, she caught it by the back of the neck and twisted sharply.

There was a satisfying crack and the struggling quieted and then ceased altogether.

All the intensity of anger and injury drained from Helena's features. With that one swift and merciless blow, she had felled both of her opponents. Denied further outlet for its hungers, the Beast within faltered, losing the scent of its prey. It sniffed the air, confused, pawing at the earth. Sharp pointed ears stood straight up atop its head, pivoting abruptly from side to side. It pressed its canine muzzle questioningly into the bundle of cloth that Helena still clung to, and gave an inquisitive whine.

Gently, patiently, Helena unwrapped the bundle and looked down upon the broken heap of feathers in her arms. She poked and prodded it., and was rewarded with a slight, but unmistakable, flutter of life beneath her questing fingertips. It was faint, but steady. Helena raised the bird to eye level, pinning its wings to its sides with one hand, and her gaze bore into its own.

Slowly, as if drawing back a hood, Helena let the Beast draw nearer to the surface. Its strength was all that was keeping her on her feet at this point. She feared that if it withdrew altogether, they all might be lost.

The jackal peeked out through her eyes as if her own features were nothing more than some elaborate and ceremonial mask. It grinned down upon the fragile little bird. With one snap of its powerful jaws, it could take her, gulp her down easily. It held that moment, savoring the prey's dawning realization of its own end. This was the apex of the hunt and the jackal reveled in it—a cycle as old and sacred and regular as the progression of day and night. How many souls had it ushered across that final threshold?

But a flicker of doubt spoiled the moment. It was something in the prey's eyes. A distracting flicker. The jackal drew closer to squelch it. It was the look of shock within the bird's eyes. It was not the alarm of its own onrushing death, but something else. The shock of recognition. Gazing full upon the face of the jackal, Antigone seemed to recognize it for the first time and, through it, Helena.

And then to remember herself. She tumbled backward, falling into her own form. Helena stumbled under the unexpected weight, lowering the girl's body as gently as possible to the floor.

They were both still for a long while, novice-hawk stretched out full length upon the marble floor, the jackal-adept stooped over her, torn between the twin needs of trying to revive her young protégée and that of starting directly in on the business of the inevitable—the dividing of the corpse. Neither impulse seemed to have the clear upper hand. Helena sat back upon her haunches and waited in the stillness.

After what seemed a long while, Antigone's eyes fluttered open. "Helena," she called weakly. And then all uncertainty was gone. The adept was there. Fully herself for the first time in many weeks.

"I'm here, Novicia. Help is coming. Be still."

Antigone laughed weakly, a sound more like a cough. "Always running, that's what he said. That I was always running."

"What who said?" Helena asked distractedly. She seemed to take in the details of the room for the first time. The broken furniture, the snapped fan, the subtly altered chalk *diagramma*. The body of Master Ynnis lying motionless on the sofa.

"The Guardian. Anubis. The Jack—" she broke off, looking uncertainly at Helen.

The adept frowned down at her. "You've had a bad shock. But you're going to be all right."

Antigone shook her off and pushed herself up to her elbows. "*I've* had a bad shock? When I found you, you were already one foot in the grave. And that was before I...um, I think you took a blow to the head," she recovered.

The adept frowned. "Yes, I seem to recall something of the sort. But we will overlook that for now." She reached out to touch the gaping wound that was once the novice's forehead. She seemed to be struggling to recall hazy details. Her voice fell to a hesitant whisper. "Did I do that?"

"Yes!" Antigone retorted angrily before falling off to mumbling. "Well, your damned warding did, which is near enough the same thing."

"Lie still. I'm fairly sure that I've...that *you've* broken your neck."

"Don't flatter yourself. It was broken when I came in here. You think I would have let you get the drop on me if I could see over my own shoulder?" Antigone rolled her head around in a slow circle, accompanied by a sharp series of crackings and poppings. "Yep, that hurts."

"Since you won't lie still," Helena began disapprovingly, "and since your neck doesn't seem to be broken after all, why don't you see if you can stand up."

Antigone took the proffered hand and hauled herself uncertainly to her feet. The room swayed, but soon righted itself. Then the words poured out of her. "I'm fine. Really. But there are folks in serious trouble. In the novice *domicilium*. You need to override the security daemon and reboot the system. There's some kind of renegade spirit on the loose and it's burning the place down...." Seeing the look on the adept's face, she fell silent.

Helena shook her head sadly. "I'm done running things. I'm done running. This is my place. This is where I belong. She needs me. It's all right if you don't understand," Helena added.

"Look, the system's locked me out. It won't respond to anybody but you or Sturbridge. If you don't shut down the system, folks are going to die. Novices are going to die."

Again Helena shook her head. "Johanus can override the system. His beth-level codes give him master access whenever Sturbridge and I are unavailable. You should know that."

"Johanus isn't here, all right?! I don't know where he is. He hasn't been back in weeks. Last I heard he was working with that swarm of refugees and transients flooding into the city. For all I know, he might be dead."

"Have you told the system that?" Helena asked calmly.

"Have I what? No, of course I haven't. Who's had time to tell the system anything? The chantry is on fire. Novices are trapped and dying in the *domicilium*. The emergency response team is pinned down. The defense network is malfunctioning. In a rare moment of clarity, it managed to take itself offline, which is likely to force an evacuation of the chantry, but that might just be the most productive thing that anyone has done about this mess. Oh yeah, and it looks like you may have killed the resident physician. You and the regent have locked yourselves in here, shut down the communications nodes and damned near blown my sorry butt up for having the effrontery to bust in and suggest that one of you might do something about this. And you're asking me if I've had the chance to report Johanus missing?"

"Here, you're obviously upset, allow me. User status change: Sturbridge, Regentia. Wounded in line of duty, torpid. Full report to follow. Delegated to Antigone, Novicia. System to monitor vital signs and reactivate clearance upon revivification. Confirm."

"Checking clearance. Helena, Adepta, gimel-level clearance. Access granted. User status change: Sturbridge, Regentia. Confirmed."

"Thank you," Helena continued. "User status change: Johanus, Adeptus. Missing in action. Full report to follow. Delegated to Antigone, Novicia. Reactivate clearance only upon return of Adeptus. Confirm."

"User status change: Johanus, Adeptus. Confirmed."

Once again Helena called, "User status change: Helena, Adepta. Resignation of duties as head of security. No further documentation available. Revert to aleph-level clearance. Confirm."

"User status change: Helena, Adepta. Confirmed."

Antigone couldn't believe her ears. "You what? You can't resign! Haven't you heard a thing I've been telling you? We're *dying* out there. We need you!"

"You don't need me, Antigone," Helena replied softly. "*She* needs me."

"You've lost it. You've all freaking lost it! Am I the only one left around here who gives a damn if the whole chantry burns to the ground?"

"You can handle this, Antigone. I'm sure of it. I have to go now. If you need me, you will know where to find me. I'll be waiting for you."

"Well that's great. Except for one thing. I don't know how to use the damned diagram! But that's fine. 'Cause you know what? I don't want to use it. You just go ahead and lock yourself into the regent's sanctum. You can stay there until the chantry burns down for all I care. But listen to me. You're going to have to feed, sooner or later. And when you do—when that *thing* takes control of you—who's going to protect Sturbridge from you then?"

Helena shook her head sadly. "You're right. You're going to have to hunt for me, I'm afraid."

"Like hell I am! I'd rather see you dead first."

"Given your activities since entering this hall, I find that difficult to believe."

"Screw you," Antigone turned her back on the adepta and stormed toward the door, all the more furious because she knew the adepta was right.

She was nearly there when she wheeled upon Helena once again, as if some further rebuke had occurred to her. "So what the hell am I supposed to do to override the damned system failure?"

Helena smiled, stepped into the chalk circle and vanished. It was not her voice that answered Antigone.

"Verifying access. Aleph-level. Highest surviving clearance status in present hierarchy. Vocal confirmation required to override."

"Antigone, Novicia. Acting head of security, lord help us." Antigone fumed. "Now shut down that damned alarm."

The klaxons fell silent.

"Reboot security grid. Emergency Response Team, report!" she called.

After only a moment a crackling voice cut in. "We can't hold it. And it sounds as if the defensive grid has finally burned itself out. We're going to have to implement the evacuation plan, and fast."

"Like hell we are," Antigone retorted. "We're cutting our losses. You've got exactly thirty seconds to get everyone out of that room and the adjoining corridor. Do you understand?"

She could hear the cries of "Go! Go! Go!" coming through the com port. She counted silently. She gave them forty-five seconds.

"Seal access corridor to novice *domicilium* and depressurize." She could hear the whoosh of air, the sudden last-ditch flare up of the flames and the first unmistakable screams. They drove the full implications of her orders home to her.

"And for God's sake, shut down that damned com port," she muttered, stalking angrily from the room.

Chapter 18
A Dozen Young Achilleses

Antigone pounded angrily down the nearly deserted corridors. After assuring herself that Master Ynnis was all right and escorting him to the infirmary, she could not bear the thought of waiting around for the rest of the emergency response teams to check back in. She was not sure she could face them right now.

There would be too many questions and too much second guessing. Antigone had condemned three novices to certain death in the burning *domicilium*. It was not something she needed to be reminded of right now. Right now what she needed was some time to put all the pieces together—to let her mind catch up to the bizarre series of transformations she had been through this evening. She needed some space to think and to rest and to heal.

There was a time, she reflected ruefully, when the thought of healing had conjured up images of sinking into the oblivion of an overstuffed feather bed, of mountains of pillows and quilts, of liberal doses of ginger ale and steaming homemade soup. Now the word invoked only images of the hunt—stalking impatiently through the early pre-dawn haze, the sound of quickened footsteps, the smell of fear, the hot rush of stolen life's blood.

Somehow, she could not bring herself to go out tonight, to force herself through the motions of the familiar rite. The reproach on the face of a stranger—an unfamiliar victim of her summary judgment—would be no better than the look on the faces of the security teams.

Instead, she made her way down to the refectory. It was deserted, which came as a relief. She kept playing over the events of the evening in her mind. She couldn't seem to shake free of them. Right up to her parting with Helena in the Hall of Audience.

Then you must hunt for me.

Damn her and her presumption. The worst part of it was that the adepta knew that Antigone would do just that—would keep Helena alive despite her best efforts to starve herself. It was more than just a matter of obeying a direct command from her superior, or even of looking out for a member of her own team. Antigone needed Helena. Needed to know what the hell was going on around here. Needed to understand the adept's strange compulsion to stand vigil over the fallen regent—even at the expense of Helena's own well-being. Damn her.

Antigone rummaged around under the cabinets until she came upon a large tartan-patterned thermos. Opening it, she crossed to the larder.

As the door swung back, the familiar stench washed over her. She batted her way through the thick cloud of midges. From the ceiling hung a dozen young Achilleses—suspended by their heels by means of stainless steel hooks.

Pressing a sleeve to her face, she made her way along the line of fragrant and pendulous fruits, looking for a ripe one. They were easy to pick out by their telltale teardrop shape—legs and abdomen stretched taut, stringy like a winter hare. The juices and tender organs puddled downward with time, collecting in and swelling the chest cavity, rendering them full, bulbous, luscious. In the very ripest ones, even the organs had begun to soften, to go to pulp.

Dispassionately, Antigone prodded a likely prospect, testing its firmness, its heft, the pulsing warmth just beneath the skin. It was ripe, alive. Perfect. Antigone's free hand snaked out, neatly catching one of the nest of wriggling white leeches that depended from the succulent flesh. It was a good foot and a half long and writhed in her grasp. She bore down hard, sending a stream of hot blood shooting into the thermos. The young Greek hero shuddered ecstatically.

It took no more than a minute to coax out a full quart of the steaming, sustaining broth. Antigone screwed the lid of the thermos back down tightly and made her way from the room.

The entire way down to the regent's sanctum, Antigone kept feeling the weight of eyes and fresh reproaches on her back. At each turning, she dreaded a chance meeting. She walked briskly, staring rigidly ahead, until she found herself at last before the imposing steel-reinforced door to the regent's sanctum.

She hoped what Helena had said about the security command hierarchy were true. If it were, there should not be a single door in the chantry—not even this imposing portal—that was barred to her.

"Open the door," she called to no one in particular.

There was a hiss of hydraulic bolts being drawn back, and the massive door swung inward. The scene inside was one of carnage. Tables were overturned. The bedcurtains had been ripped from the canopy, bundled up in a great blood-stained wad, and cast into one corner. The computer terminal lay on the floor, its face shattered and still sparking.

A bone-piercing cold hung over the entire scene. Antigone let out a slow breath and watched as it instantly condensed into a delicate pink-tinged cloud. Long, spear-like icicles hung from the cast-iron canopy.

Neither of the other two figures in the room turned, or made any sign to acknowledge her entrance. Helena sat on the floor, rigid, upright—to all appearances, vigilant. Her body held the mountain pose reflexively. Even the weight of her wounds and the fundamental schism that she had wrought upon herself could not crush her body's instinctive physical discipline.

But Antigone could see that the adept's head slumped forward and she was now oblivious to all around her. Helena was deep in the grips of restorative torpor—secure in her belief that the security system would keep out any who would intrude upon her. And that her charge would pose no further threat.

Sturbridge lay insensate on the bed. She did not stir, and her skin had an unhealthy bluish tinge to it. One arm draped over the edge of the bed, bent at an unnatural angle. And protruding from her chest, a gleaming crimson stake.

Antigone suppressed a cry. Cautiously, she crept closer to the fallen regent. When last she had seen Sturbridge, the regent had been torpid from her encounter in the crypts. But this spike was certainly a new development. It spoke of some further struggle. Some further attempt on her life.

Antigone picked her way past Helena, careful not to disturb the adepta, and bent over the fallen regent. A shard of ice, as long as a railroad spike, jutted defiantly from Sturbridge's breast. It seemed to be composed entirely of frozen blood. As Antigone watched, a single crimson droplet condensed, beaded and slid languidly downward.

Her mind reeled with questions, but her hand instinctively reached out to act. Her fingers closed upon the spike.

She felt its pervading cold, felt the ice sink its teeth into the flesh of her fingertips and hold fast. Bracing her free hand upon the regent's shoulder, she gave a great heave.

The spike slid free with the wet tearing sound of tissue parting. Sturbridge sat bolt upright, her vision filled with the sight of the upraised stake in Antigone's hand. The regent bared long, wicked fangs.

Antigone stumbled back, nearly precipitating herself to the floor. But Sturbridge's eyes followed her, dogged her. Antigone could not shake free of the intensity of that gaze. Behind it, she could see the surging of the Beast. It threw its head back and reared. Two massive hooves—each easily as large as Antigone's head—rent the air mere inches from her face. Both were shod with glyphs of sizzling neon.

She wanted to drop the stake. Wanted it desperately. As much as she could remember ever wanting anything in the world. Her fingers opened, but the ice shard clung tenaciously to her skin. She tried distractedly to shake free of it as her other arm came up—- as if mere flesh and bone could hope to ward off those flashing hooves.

Antigone felt the skin of her fingertips rip away as the crimson spike tore free and skidded across the icy floor. She sank to her knees, head bent before the twin crushing blows that must surely follow.

But the mercy stroke did not fall.

Summoning her courage, Antigone peered up and met her regent's eyes. The rearing war-horse was gone. Instead there was only the chill calm of dark subterranean waters.

"That was a very foolish thing to do, Novicia." Sturbridge's voice rang hollow, distant, emotionless. It sounded as if it were echoing up from the depths of a cistern.

"I am sorry, Regentia. I did not think. I…"

"Sorry?" Sturbridge's eyes seemed to focus on the novice for the first time. The sense of vast distances and chill caverns was gone, replaced by a hint of something more human. Amusement?

"What I meant to say is…" Antigone began, but Sturbridge laid a hand upon her shoulder. Antigone fell silent.

"Apology accepted." This time there was a genuine smile. Sturbridge raised Antigone to her feet. "It was a foolish thing to do, but I, for one, am grateful that you did so. I doubt the adepta would share this opinion." Sturbridge looked across to where Helena sat, her back to them, her pose of alertness belying the extent of her hurt.

"But how did…who has done this?" Antigone demanded.

"Be easy now, little one," Sturbridge said. Antigone started at the familiarity. She knew that someone else had called her by this name recently, but she could not quite place who or where. "All in good time. I said that the adepta would not approve of your actions because she thought it best that I be subdued for a time. I cannot bring myself to blame her. I've made something of a mess of things lately and Helena assumes—not without cause—that I have gone mad. And she has been hurt recently. Deeply hurt. And I am not entirely blameless in that matter either."

Antigone did not know what to make of this pronouncement. If the regent had become unstable, then it was Helena's duty, as head of security, to make sure that Sturbridge did not harm herself or others. A duty which now fell to Antigone. With a slow-dawning apprehension, Antigone began to get a sense that she might just have made a very big mistake. Her eyes darted across the room to where the frozen spike had come to rest.

Sturbridge caught her sideways glance. "What do *you* think?" she asked the novice.

Antigone took her time, choosing her words very carefully. "I think you are both hurt far worse than you're willing to admit. Helena was nearly gone when I found her—at war with herself. You weren't much better off. I thought you were dead just now. I don't pretend to know why Helena thought you had…that you had become unstable. I don't much care…."

"She believes that I killed Eva," Sturbridge supplied. "And perhaps other novices as well. And that I have eaten their flesh."

This last revelation brought Antigone up short. "That you *what*?"

"I know. It sounds silly, really, when you just say it outright like that. But Helena knows that Eva is gone. And she knows the Children are gone. And Helena has been hurt very deeply."

Antigone's head was swimming. "I don't understand," she said. "I don't understand any of this. Are you trying to tell me that *Helena* has become unstable? That she just attacked you? That this all has something to do with the day the nightmares stopped?"

Sturbridge smiled. "No. That is very perceptive, but I'm trying to tell you almost the exact opposite. Helena has strong evidence for her understandable but mistaken impression that I have become unhinged. She suffered a deep hurt the day the nightmares stopped, but that injury is not simply psychological. It is very real. I can smell the blood upon her even now. And the nightmares have not stopped, not really. Not for all of us."

"You still see them?" Antigone craned forward eagerly. "The Children? Then they are not destroyed! But what does it mean? Why can you still see them, but no one else can?"

"What do you think the Children are, Antigone?" Sturbridge's gaze was intense, penetrating.

Antigone shrugged self-consciously. "I don't know. They are just a nightmare, a recurring nightmare. I thought it was just me at first. But then I found out that Helena had seen them too. And now you! I think there are others, but no one will admit to it. Nobody wants to talk about it. Everyone wants to just sort of pretend it all never happened. But how can two people share the same nightmare? Or three people? Or..."

"Or all of us," Sturbridge said.

"All of us?" Antigone could not seem to reconcile the concept to the behavior of the others. "Everyone in the whole chantry?!"

"All of our people," Sturbridge replied. "In every chantry. Even those outside a chantry. The lost, the fallen, the forgotten. The traitors and renegades; the bastards and byblows. All who share in the blood are complicit in the nightmare."

"But how can that be?" Antigone challenged. "How can you dream my nightmare?"

"Because it's not your nightmare, Antigone. It's not my nightmare, although I am now its vessel. It's the nightmare of the Father. The blood is its conduit, just as it is the conduit of our magic. His power reaches out through us and remakes the world in His image. Look at your hand."

Antigone gave Sturbridge a puzzled look, but then stared down at her torn fingertips. The blood was welling to the surface, seeping through dozens of minute tears too tiny even to distinguish.

"Our Father's nightmare bleeds out into the world through you. You are its conduit. You rise each evening and open your eyes upon our Father's nightmare. You sink into fitful slumber each morning and close your eyes upon our Father's nightmare. Only the most ephemeral of barriers separates the two worlds — it is no more formidable than the thickness of an eyelid. You and I, we are the creatures of that dream — its creations — utterly and completely. Waking or sleeping, there is no escaping it, nor denying its power, its vision. It is what we are."

Antigone shook her head in denial. What Sturbridge was saying could not be true. It was monstrous, blasphemous, too much to take in.

Sturbridge's voice was calm and steadying. "Novicia, I am going to ask you a hard question. It is one someone should have put to you a long time ago. That this was not done, I am truly sorry. Under different circumstances...without the nightly pressures of the Sabbat siege, perhaps — some things, some vitally important things, would not have gone so long unsaid and undone. We will yet pay the price of these sins of omission. But I will put a question to you.

"Why is it that the power of the blood comes readily to some of us and not to others? Why some can labor away for decades without managing to tap the raw power and potential inherent in the blood?"

Antigone's eyes burned with shame. She would not meet her regent's stare. "You know that I cannot answer your question, Regentia," Antigone said bitterly.

"Then I will tell you why. It is fear. Fear chokes off the very flow of the life-giving blood—the raw power of it, the magic, the majesty. The neophyte shies away from the Father's nightmare—from its dark hungers, its bitter recriminations. If you cannot face the Children, Antigone, the dark side of our gift, then you cannot hope to work the debased miracles of the blood magics."

"How can I face them?" Antigone's voice was a desperate whisper. She did not look up. "How can anyone face them? They are gone. Lost to us. You have said so yourself. When I close my eyes, there is only the darkness—damning in its mundanity. And I am alone."

Sturbridge made no answer. In silence, she turned her forearm upward and ran a razor-sharp fingernail from elbow to wrist. Only the slightest hint of vitae welled about the edges of the gash. As Antigone watched, dark water began to seep from the open wound.

Chapter 19
Shepherds of the Flame

"I said that I will see Sturbridge. Immediately. And I will not be put off." Emmett struggled to haul his broken body the length of the approach to the Grande Foyer. He was obviously distraught as well as severely wounded. If, on the Nosferatu's previous visit to the chantry, Talbott had found him terrible to behold, Emmett had clearly outdone himself on this occasion. Fresh and disfiguring burns covered half of his face and stretched around to encompass the back of his bald pate. His scalp looked as if it had been seared smooth rather than shaved. One arm was withered to a useless and blackened stump. Emmett kept the maimed limb pressed tightly against his chest.

He wore the tattered remains of an old and stained surplus blanket clutched tightly around his shoulders with his remaining hand. Beneath it he wore a coarse knee-length shirt which seemed to be woven entirely of human hair. It was hastily belted with a thick rope tied in the front like a noose. On his feet, he wore torn blue rubber flip-flops.

"I'm very sorry," Talbott said with remarkable calm. "As I mentioned on your visit of last night, the regent is unavailable for at least another fortnight. The prince somehow dissatisfied with the regent's response?"

"The prince currently lies dying. An assassin..." Emmett blurted out defiantly and immediately broke off, sorry that he had been goaded into speaking at all.

Talbott was unshaken. "I see. That is grave news indeed. And the dying prince has summoned my mistress to his bedside? To receive his final blessing, or perhaps, the name of his murderer?"

"There is no time to delay," Emmett replied. "She must come at once or all might be lost. You will take me to her. Now."

Talbott saw the steel in his glance. There was no delicate way to put off such a request. "I will conduct you immediately to the Hall of Audience. Will you be so kind as to follow me?"

Emmett, taken aback by this sudden acquiescence, muttered something inarticulate and gestured for the gatekeeper to lead on before he had a chance to change his mind.

"You must stay close to me," Talbott called over his shoulder. "I would hate to lose you to a misstep in the dark." He ducked beneath a jet of blazing blue flame and continued without hesitation.

Emmett, however, recoiled sharply, his eyes wide in the presence of the ancient adversary. The wounds from their recent meeting were still too fresh in his mind — and not only in his mind. He drew his withered arm more deeply into the recesses of the army blanket, hiding it from sight.

Emmett could feel the unreasoning panic tugging at him again, surging up within him. It had a life of its own — a soul forged in rage; a will tempered beneath the hammer of desperation. The creature bellowed like some grotesque primeval boar that, having been cornered and held at spearpoint, turned upon the presumptuous hunter in an unquenchable red fury. Emmett's oversized teeth scissored wetly, snapping well out beyond the line of his jaw. Twin rows of curved yellow tusks. He threw back his head and howled defiance. His good hand slammed down upon the blackened cast-iron pipe that fed the blaze. It burst with a squeal of metal, a vindictive hissing, and the clatter and bounce of three different pipe sections spinning across the floor.

Talbott turned in alarm and managed to yell, "Get down!" before the entire scene before him erupted in inferno.

Emmett, for his part, needed no prompting. He was running purely on instinct and the surging tides of the blood now. Where they coursed, he had no choice but to follow.

He rolled heavily to one side, evading the brunt of the blast that rocked the room. With a grunt, he pushed himself back to his feet, but did not straighten to his full height. He crouched, shielded behind a bank of copper pipes, each as thick around as his chest. He could see the metal fittings had already begun to bubble and melt. For the second time in as many nights, he had narrowly managed to slip the ancient foe's best shot.

A spear-thrust of blue flame flared to his left. He spun, catching the thick metal haft and twisting. The pipe groaned and bent, the spearhead of flame jabbing harmlessly upward.

He could no longer see his guide, Talbott. He was cut off by the rearing walls of brass and flame. Emmett leapt over a clutch of flaming serpents that hissed and sputtered at his passing. He caught onto an overhead pipe and clung fast. With apparent effort, he hauled himself upward with his one good arm and squatted atop the precarious perch, surveying the nightmarish gasworks below.

Dark cowled figures scurried in and amongst the flames. They wrestled with oversized brass valves, trying to control the unchecked inferno. No, that wasn't quite right. The more he watched them, the more Emmett became convinced that they were actually feeding the flames, tending them, shepherding them. They drove the gouts of fire from shadowed pasture to shadowed pasture, along the well-worn tracks of copper piping and brass nozzles.

It was the purpose behind this flurry of activity, however, that eluded him.

"Emmett, you must come down immediately! We will never be able to win through to the Hall of Audiences if you cannot reign in the Beast. Please come down."

Emmett snarled something that might have been, "Then make them shut down the gas main! And then send them away. Send them all away!"

Talbot looked around hopelessly. All around him, the damage control teams struggled to check the runaway nightmare of flame, to stop Emmett before he caused himself lasting harm. Judging from his appearance and his wild tales of assassinations, he had surely suffered enough within the last twenty-four hours.

"They are attempting to do exactly that," the gatekeeper replied. "Only you have to let them. The Grande Foyer feeds upon each desire, or its converse, each fear. If you surrender to the Beast in here, we will surely have to incapacitate you to bring you out again. Do you understand me?"

Emmett's sole reply was to swing down into the very midst of the nearest knot of scurrying robed figures, scattering them. He ducked low, and flames whooshed above him. He turned a corner, diving into the relative safety of a shadowed recess, only to freeze a moment later, rooted to the spot by a seductive hissing that tickled his ear.

Somewhere, Talbott was calling his name, but Emmett was in no hurry to be pinned down again. He had to avoid detection and the deadly scrutiny that was its inevitable consequence. He had to find his own way through.

He remembered bits and pieces of the true path from his previous visit. But all these pipes and valves and levers must have been part of some newer installation. Everything had been grossly and inexplicably rearranged. He could see no purpose, no grand design behind the labyrinth of flame and shadow. It was a monumental achievement, a daunting edifice, but its purpose eluded him.

At times it seemed to him that he was lost in the very bowels of the chantry. A vast undercity of pipes, ducts, conduits and steam tunnels that supported and sustained...what exactly? The chantry house? The university? The city itself? It was an infrastructure seeking expression. Searching doggedly for its twin, its aboveground complement, that might make it whole, give it purpose.

At other times, he thought he was deep within the holy of holies, the innermost tabernacle dedicated to the stunted god of secrets and searing revelations. The dark one was fickle and teasing, hinting at favors never quite realized, granting gifts never quite asked for.

And at other times, he thought he was in no edifice that was ever made by the hands of man at all. This high bank of feeder pipes was surely the ridge of a hill. The treacherous, exposed path along the sea cliffs was fit only for the scrawny sure-footed goats that haunted those desolate heights. The fishermen in the village below called the path the Widow's Walk. And it was said that if a fishwife could carry a basin brimming full of water to its summit—without spilling a single drop—then when the rising moon was reflected there, it would reveal to her what the sea would bring her and her children the next day. Mysteries within mysteries.

Somewhere here, amidst the tangle of unnamed fields and forking paths, was the central fountain where he had met Sturbridge on that other visit. It all seemed somehow so far removed now. But Emmett knew if he could only win through to the fountain, all would be well.

With a squeal of metallic protest, the bank of pipes atop which he crouched gave way beneath his weight. He fell heavily to the floor, amidst a clatter of copper pipes, each as wide around as the bole of a tree. They ushered him into the darkened undercity of oblivion.

The last sound he heard before the walls of that dark city closed over him was a familiar voice. Or was it only a final trick of the Grande Foyer—taunting him with one further desire?

"It is all right, Emmett," Sturbridge said, cradling the fallen Nosferatu's head in her lap. "I am here."

Chapter 20
Ms. Blackbird

"I am pleased that you have come to us for sanctuary, Mr. Felton. We have been following your exploits with great interest. If you will follow me, I will show you to your cell."

A look like that of a cornered animal flickered across his features. He quickly checked his path to the exit, knowing it was already too late. He had crossed a threshold. He was within the domain of the warlocks.

Antigone smiled reassuringly. "I should say, your quarters. We use the word 'cell' in the monastic sense here, to indicate a private room as opposed to a *domicilium* for a group of novices. We are not your jailers, Mr. Felton. You have nothing to fear on that account."

Felton shifted uncomfortably. "No, of course not. It was…a kindness of you to take me in." His voice was little more than a whisper. The events of the last two nights were beginning to take their toll upon him. He needed rest and he needed to feed and he needed a little time to piece things together. The echo of his words returned to him and he unconsciously drew the cowl further down over his face. The robes were coarse and itchy where they rubbed against his skin. He kept his head bent low.

"Not at all," she said. With a swirl of long skirts she turned and strode off toward the center of the Grande Foyer, without pausing to see if he followed. "I myself have taken an active interest in your case. Does that surprise you? We are not so cloistered here as you might think. It seems you have become something of a celebrity, Mr. Felton. Nineteen million people, in this town alone, would like nothing better than to see you dead. That's quite an accomplishment."

Felton, who had been half jogging to catch up with her, stopped cold. He was not sure how to take this 'compliment.' He recognized that his position here was precarious. If his hosts should decide that he was more trouble than he was worth, the best he could hope for was to be unceremoniously expelled and left to fend for himself again on the street. There were, however, far less promising scenarios. Being turned over to the police or to the prince sprang to mind. He decided that his safest bet would be to take everything his hosts might say at face value and in return to be as frank as he could. "I agree. Quite an accomplishment. And I'd very much like to meet the guy who engineered it. I have some questions I'd like to ask him."

She glanced back at him out of the corner of her eye. "I was just thinking much the same thing. But you are being far too humble. False modesty ill-suits those in your line of work."

"My line of work?" he asked, not liking where this line of inquiry was going.

"Terrorists. Mercenaries. Freedom fighters, if you prefer, as I understand that some of you do. It makes little difference to me. I am not here to be your judge, Mr. Felton."

"I am grateful for that," he said, perhaps a touch too earnestly. "But I'm no terrorist, Ms. Baines. I didn't set off that bomb. But I'm going to find out who did."

"And clear your name. Yes, I do believe that's the traditional approach. But not tonight, perhaps. I think it might be best for you to withdraw into seclusion for a time. You will find that this house is uniquely suited to that very purpose. Let the outside world proceed apace without you."

"I thank you for your hospitality. I realize you are taking a risk just to have me here. I do not know how I will return the favor."

"You may rest easy on that score. We would be poor hosts indeed were we to allow any guest to leave here feeling that he was in our debt. If it would make you feel better, I am sure we could find some way for you to earn your keep during your stay. But not tonight."

They walked in silence for a time, Felton trying to figure what benefit the Tremere could possibly get out of this. The situation was politically charged. If the prince's goons were to learn that the chantry was sheltering him, there would be trouble. And not just for Felton. If the situation were reversed, if this young Tremere were in a jam, Felton wouldn't have thought twice. He would have kept his head down. That's what he was trained to do under fire.

"Can I ask you a question? What do you guys—" Felton began.

She surprised him by interrupting. He had asked permission only as a formality. "Certainly, Mr. Felton. You may ask me anything you like. Answers are not, however, part of your arrangement with this House. Please be aware they may cost extra."

"Hmm. Well, that's just it. I don't really have a formal arrangement. I just told that gatekeeper guy that I needed sanctuary—"

"Sanctuary is a very formal arrangement, Mr. Felton. One with a tradition stretching back well over a thousand years. Would it surprise you to learn that House Tremere has defended this tradition in the face of the wrath of popes and emperors? We have steadfastly repulsed the best efforts of Tzimisce inquisitors and Assamite fanatics. It is an obligation we take very seriously."

"I didn't mean anything like that," Felton protested. "I just needed a place to lie low for a while. You know, until this whole thing settles down and I can start looking for the guy who really set off that bomb. I only came here because Char—" Felton checked himself, realizing he might well be saying too much by dragging Charlie's name into this. He changed gears abruptly. "*I was told* that if I presented myself here and asked for sanctuary that you would take me in. That you wouldn't turn me over to the police or the prince's men. That was all I meant. I don't know anything about any ancient rite. I've heard about all this blood-magic stuff, of course. Who hasn't? But..."

"Sanctuary is not a thaumaturgic ritual, Mr. Felton. It is a social convention. I assure you, it is quite painless. And, seeing as you have already placed yourself under our protection, there is really no point in developing qualms about the arrangement at this point."

"But what if I—intending no disrespect, of course—but what if I'm not happy with the arrangement? What if things just don't work out? What if I can't live up to my end of the deal? I really don't know anything about your customs and traditions. What happens when it's time for me to pay my tab and go?"

"Mr. Felton, the door is always open to you. As I said, you are not our prisoner. If you wish to terminate our protection, you need only walk out the front door. Please note, however, that by leaving the chantry you effectively absolve us from any further obligation to you. For example, if you again presented yourself on our doorstep, we would be under no compulsion to take you back in."

"I see," Felton said. "That's more what I was expecting. Are there any other conditions I should know about?"

"Any communication with the outside world will be construed as a termination of our arrangement. That includes telephone, fax, mail, e-mail, *et cetera*. You will not receive any visitors during your stay, lest they inadvertently compromise your position."

"I'm glad you cleared up that bit about not being in prison right off the bat," Felton said.

Antigone ignored him. "You will follow all the rules of this house. The Master of Novices is away at the moment, but I will have one of the senior apprentices drop in this evening and fill you in on what is expected of you. Basically, you are now an oblate, a lay student. Your course of studies will be traditional: the Trivium—grammar, logic, rhetoric. Don't worry, nothing esoteric. We'll hold off on the obsidian knives and still-beating hearts for the present. That is, unless…"

Felton felt he was being teased, but decided not to take any chances. "No, that will be fine. The classics. Although I'm not much of a…what did you call it?"

"An oblate. Now, you should be aware that the regular novices are not going to want to have anything to do with you. Their proximity to the very foot of the hierarchy tends to make them rabidly class-conscious. I would be very suspicious of anyone who does show an interest."

Antigone paused, reflecting for a moment upon the purity of her own reasons for taking in the saboteur, and finding them wanting. She purposefully avoided any reference to her own station. Although she was, at present, the acting head of security, she herself was a mere novice—and of the very lowest circle. It was a station from which decades of exemplary service had been unable to extricate her. Although she had been rapidly promoted within the security team, Antigone found herself consistently passed over for advancement within the Pyramid. Position, prestige and class-consciousness at the chantry were never so black and white as she was painting them.

Realizing the uncomfortable silence, Antigone pressed on. "The Chantry of Five Boroughs is a war chantry, Mr. Felton. These novices have only been assigned here because they have already demonstrated that they do not play nicely with others. I trust you understand me. It's probably best for you to steer clear of the regular novices as much as possible. If you keep to yourself and limit your excursions to the library, the refectory, and other non-recreational common areas, you should get along just fine."

"Ms. Baines, I've been going toe-to-toe with the Sabbat for well over a decade now. You don't need to have any fears on my account. I can handle myself in a precarious situation."

"That's is exactly why I am telling you this, Mr. Felton. I would not want you to be deceived by the orderliness of your surroundings. It would be a mistake—and quite possibly a final mistake—to think that a clutch of novices at their studies was any less deadly than a rampaging Sabbat warpack."

"I thank you for the warning," Felton said. "I think I will keep largely to my chamber, if it's all the same to you. Will I take classes with the other oblates or are they as ravenous as the novices?"

"Not nearly so. Most of them are actually presentable enough that they can take a few classes at the college above. But I do not think we will run any unnecessary risks with you for the present. We will arrange a private tutor."

"So all I have to do is stay put, avoid all contact with anyone outside, mind my manners and keep to myself. And, so long as I do, I can stay as long as I like. And I don't have to worry about being volunteered for any sort of blood rite?"

"That's the basic gist of it, yes. Now, is there anything you particularly need to have with you during your stay? It would be best, of course, if you were to have no personal possessions about you whatsoever. Clothing, jewelry, photos, weapons and wallet are obviously right out. They carry strong signatures and are far too easy to trace. It would probably be better if you were shaved and your nails plucked as well, but we certainly won't force the issue."

"That's very kind of you. I think I'll opt out of that one under the no-blood-rites clause." Felton considered. "I don't think there's anything special I need. I can get my clothes and papers and stuff back when I leave, right?"

"It would be better for them to be destroyed." Antigone said.

"You guys aren't fooling around about all this are you? All right, burn the clothes. But there are some papers I am going to need back if I'm ever going to clear my name."

"I will have them cleared and brought to you this evening."

"What do you mean, 'cleared'? I don't want anybody rummaging through my—"

"No one is going to read your papers, Mr. Felton. Not in the sense you are using. I meant that I will have a sensitive scan the folder for resonances. She should be able to mute out or mask any dangerous signatures. With a bit of luck and a weekly retouch, that should do to block any sympathetic magics. We wouldn't want anyone targeting you by using the evidence that you hope will redeem you."

"Why does it sound like things have only gotten more dangerous since I arrived here?"

"They have, but not for you, Mr. Felton. You need not fear any outside threat while you are with us."

"Yeah, I get it. Only the inside threats, right?"

"I think we understand each other. As long as you follow the guidelines we have established, I am sure we will all get along just fine. Ah, here we are now."

She paused before a simple wooden door which stood slightly ajar. She whisked into the room ahead of him and switched on the desk lamp—the only source of light in the tiny cell. She ran a critical gaze over the arrangements. Bed, desk, chair and washstand took up the vast majority of the cramped space. There was already a considerable pile of books laid in.

Felton squeezed around her and sat on the edge of the bed. With satisfaction, he noted the lack of a window or any other means of ingress. "This will be great, thanks. I guess I'll just catch up on my reading then."

She caught his gaze checking the exit. "The door latches on the inside, but it is really just a formality. I only mention it because a number of the novices pride themselves on their lockpicking skills. Since you have next to no personal possessions—and will be going to great pains to avoid antagonizing the novices—these little intrusions should not greatly inconvenience you. Once their initial curiosity is frustrated, they will likely abandon you as a waste of effort. At any rate, make sure to latch the door securely whenever you are in. Nothing feeds their suspicions more than an unlocked door."

"Anything else I need to watch out for, besides the novices?"

"Yes. You know what the oblate robes look like— unbleached wool. The novices wear black with a band of color at the cuffs, neckline or belt denoting rank. Anyone who is not dressed like this—for example if you see anyone wearing bright-colored or white robes—you avoid. And when I say avoid, I mean keep your head down and your cowl up. If you find yourself in the same room as one of these personages, you contrive to slip away as soon as it is polite to do so. You don't speak unless you are first spoken to. You don't turn your back on them under any circumstances, even when leaving the room."

"I understand. That's good to know. I'm not much for pretenses like rank and title, but I make it a point not to insult anybody by accident."

"A wise policy. As a guest and a supplicant, you are advised not to insult any of the luminaries of this house on purpose either." Antigone moved toward the door. "Is there anything else you require?"

Felton lowered his gaze and considered. He held her there with his reluctance to speak, unwilling perhaps to be left alone within the heart of the warlocks' domain. "Can I ask you some—" he began and then broke off. "I know, 'answers have their price.' And I also know that I am already in your debt. But what I wanted to know was if there was any way you guys could help me with finding out who set me up, who really planted that bomb."

Antigone paused, one hand on the door handle. She regarded him with the same exacting scrutiny that she had, just a moment before, turned upon the room's preparations. With her head cocked to one side, Felton thought she resembled some curious bird—a crow, sizing up the farmer intruding upon the bird's cornfield.

"Anything is possible here, Mr. Felton. But you must be very wary when trafficking in possibilities. Their price is always weighed out in blood. Earlier you seemed reluctant to have anything to do with the thaumaturgic."

Felton shivered involuntarily. "I won't lie to you. All that blood-magic stuff gives me the creeps. I've seen those damned Kolduns, seen their dark rites, seen the price they exact from their victims. But if that's the only way I can find out what I need to know, then that's what I'm going to have to do."

"I assure you, Mr. Felton, that our techniques are somewhat more...refined than those of the Tzimisce butchers. We have spent centuries coaxing out the secrets of the blood. There is very little that is hidden from us."

"Then you *can* help me. I had heard the stories, of course, but you can't exactly build up a hope—much less a plan of attack—upon rumors and old wives' tales. Tell me what I have to do. And what it will cost me. If I can pay it, I will."

"Now, that is exactly the sort of pledge that gets people in over their heads, Mr. Felton. But no matter, it cannot be withdrawn now. I expect, however, that you will endeavor to be more cautious in our future dealings. I will consider your problem—and your offer—and we will talk more of it tomorrow. Good night, Mr. Felton."

"Ms. Baines? Thank you for your help, and for the warnings. Can I ask you—I mean, I hope you will not think it impolite of me to ask. You told me about the unbleached oblate robes. And I know the novice robes are black with bands of color for the different ranks. And the masters' robes are colored or white. But you did not tell me what the plain black robes signified."

Helena felt the flush of anger and embarrassment. She looked down at her own unadorned black robes, which announced her as a novice of the first circle. Struggling to master her emotion, she replied somewhat bitterly, "It means that I am a jackal. And that some of us have nothing left to prove."

It was his turn to regard her curiously. He could see her anger and did not want to contradict her. But her statement was obviously the furthest thing from the truth. Her every gesture was that of someone trying desperate to prove herself. *A jackal,* he thought. *Not a hunter or warrior who brings down her own prey, but a scavenger. A carrion-eater. One who feeds upon the dead.*

Felton now knew what he had only begun to suspect earlier. That Antigone was not attending to him because she was some chantry dignitary, but rather quite the opposite. This duty fell to her because she was an outcast among her own kind. One who could go among mere oblates and outsiders without fear of further contamination. Ministering to the pariahs, the lepers.

An image, a favorite story from his youth, sprang unbidden to mind. He could see a man dressed in simple brown robes, standing alone in a cemetery. He was preaching a sermon to a

172 / Eric Griffin

congregation of rooks and ravens. St. Francis of Assisi. As Felton had grown older, of course, he had come to see the story in a different light. The ascetic holy man, himself an outcast, taking the word of God to the persecuted, the dispossessed, the unclean. To those no respectable man would stoop to associate himself with.

He wondered if Antigone saw her efforts in that light. If she thought of herself as a saint, a martyr. He thought of the women whose duty it was to prepare the dead for burial. In some cultures, any contact with dead flesh was thought of as a lasting contamination, a physical as well as a spiritual blemish. He could see her very easily in that light. The solemn woman draped in black robes attending, with exacting attention to detail, upon the needs of the dead and damned. He lay back on the bed and folded his hands on his chest.

Felton wondered if there were not some further hidden meaning in her simple statement, if she were not trying to tell him something. *I am a jackal.* An eater of the dead. He knew that there were those among the undying who literally fed upon others of their kind. It was the one unpardonable sin of their society. Diablerists, they were called. Those who do the work of *El Diablo*. The Devil's handmaidens. Felton regarded the severe young warlock in her long, gown-like black robes. He could picture her ministering to the dark powers as easily as he had envisioned her attending upon the recently deceased. As easily as he had seen her waiting upon himself.

Felton thought he had seen enough battlefields to recognize a jackal when he saw one. There was some aspect of the battlefield about his hostess, but of the carnage at the battle's end. She was more like some dark and predatory bird. A rook, a raven...

"You're a strange bird," he muttered.

Antigone started, remembering the black wings buffeting her face. She recalled her confrontation with the laughing

Warden of the Dead and how, when he had drawn her out of her bones, she had found herself in the body of a bird. Or had it all been a nightmare? No, Helena had raw red wounds on her face to prove both beak and talon had been quite real.

"I will look forward to your visit tomorrow night, then," Felton said. "Don't forget me, Ms. Blackbird. You made me a promise."

"You would do better to call to mind your own extravagant promises," she replied. "Good night, Mr. Felton. Try not to blow anything up. We have had far too much excitement of that sort already."

Chapter 21
The Levitating Prince

"He wants what?!" Umberto reluctantly turned away from the computer monitor and glowered. He was short-tempered and bone tired. He should have collapsed hours ago. But he couldn't allow himself to do so until after he had made damned sure that the demographic data had transferred correctly. If what Johanus said about the distribution of these population figures was true…

"A bathtub. You know, big thing. Porcelain. You fill it with water," Donatello shot back. He ducked under a bundle of electrical cable as big around as his waist that hung like a cordon across the tunnel access. He followed the course of the cabling with his eye to where it disappeared into a low rat-like tunnel in the corner. The rubber sheathing was nearly chewed through and the exposed wiring within threw sparks where it contacted a murky puddle. "You know that's gonna kill somebody sooner or later, right?"

Umberto pointedly ignored him. "I know what a bathtub is, idiot. Why the hell does Emmett want a bathtub and what's it got to do with me? Somebody die and make me the resident plumber now too?"

"Look, I just need to know if you know where I can find one. One of those free-standing numbers. You'd think with all this damned sewer piping around here, somebody might know of where I could lay hands on a bathtub. It's for the prince. Sturbridge is here and…"

"Sturbridge? The Tremere regent? She's here?" Umberto was on his feet, upsetting the metal folding chair.

"I don't know why everyone thinks that you're some kind of genius or something. Yes, Aisling Sturbridge. That's what I've been telling you. How many Sturbridges do you…never mind. Look, do you know where I can get a tub or don't you?"

"They're with the prince now?" Umberto asked.

"Yeah, Sturbridge, Emmett, a couple of folks from the chantry porting what looks like the components for some kind of still. I didn't ask. I just end up fetching the tub. Any ideas?"

"Um, yeah. One sec," Umberto turned and toggled the computer over to the inventory screens. He keyed a search. "Rag Picker's got one of those old cast-iron ones down at his place, down off the A line…."

"I know the place. Thanks!" Donatello ducked back under the cable and started up the tunnel.

"You want me to tell him to have some boys bring it up?" Umberto called after him.

That brought him up short. "Yeah…that would be great. You know, you're not half as useless as you let on. Only, tell him it's important."

"You're welcome," Umberto snorted. "And don't go anywhere until I'm done here. I'm coming with you."

The procession that descended upon the prince's lair was intended, no doubt, to be a solemn one. Umberto could not help thinking, however, that there was some unmistakable hint of the carnival about the whole affair. Sturbridge's retinue of conjurers paraded a steady stream of wooden casks, packing cases, rolls of rubber tubing, into the chamber. Slowly, they began to assemble the big top.

It was *unseemly* that so many strangers should be here. That they should stand gawking over the fallen prince was bad enough. Calebros lay on a folding army-surplus cot, covered from head to toe in a plain white sheet. A corpse. Umberto could pick out each line of the prince's ribcage, even through the sheet. He did not care to see what lay beneath.

The magicians went about their work with an ill-concealed excitement. Sturbridge, the ringmaster, directed their efforts with a gentle word here, a helping hand there. The packing cases surrendered their wonders with the flourish of a top hat sprouting rabbits. A mad alchemist's nightmare began to take form, a hanging mobile of glass alembics, copper tubing and gas burners. The entire improbable construct spun lazily upon the heat it generated.

When the Rag Picker's childer arrived, dragging the huge cast-iron bathtub, no one even batted an eye. The tub was slid into place beneath the waiting arachnid apparatus of glass, copper and rubber.

Throughout the strange process, Emmett spoke to Sturbridge in whispers, obviously apprehensive. She reassured him with her smile, confidence, and touch. At last, she said, "It is time," and nudged Emmett toward the unmoving form of the prince. He stood at the prince's head and threw Umberto a worried look. The latter immediately crossed to him and took up position at the foot of the cot. On *three*, they lifted him.

Umberto was startled at how little effort it took. He almost , but caught himself instantly. There could be little more to Calebros now than skin and bones, he reflected ruefully. Maybe not even skin.

They carried him carefully, still concealed beneath the clinging sheet, over to the great cast-iron tub. Umberto could not help thinking that this proceeding only strengthened the appearance that there was some stage magic at work here. The levitating prince. He had a momentary vision of Sturbridge stepping forward and passing a hoop over the body as if to prove that there were no strings holding it up. Any moment now, Emmett would snatch away the concealing sheet with a flourish and there would be nothing there. He would bow, Sturbridge would bow. The rest of the assembly would applaud and then file out of the chamber.

Umberto let out a sigh of relief as they laid the prince into the bottom of the tub—relief that they had completed their task without inflicting any further indignities upon their fallen leader. He stood there dumbly and was gently shouldered aside by the trio of Tremere porters who busied themselves with lowering and adjusting the strange alchemical equipment. Still he could only stand mutely and stare.

It was Sturbridge's voice that brought him out of his reverie. "You'll never work it open with that blade. It's little more than a straight razor." She turned toward Emmett. "Have you got something a bit more substantial? It is important that we get him submerged as soon as possible."

Her voice jolted Umberto into action. Like a somnambulist, he crossed to the wall, where he wrested loose a neglected and rusted fireaxe. Returning, he smiled down at the magician who was still working his razor out of the seam of the wooden cask. The other quickly stepped aside.

Umberto swung the axe with one hand, only hard enough to firmly lodge it in the top of the cask. He worked it loose only to be immediately assaulted by the reek of formaldehyde. He stepped back, shaking his head to clear it, while the nearest Tremere upended the cask over the tub.

The thick, pungent fluid gurgled and splashed onto the fallen prince. They repeated the operation three more times, until the body was completely submerged.

Sturbridge, meanwhile, was standing at one end of the tangle of alchemical equipment. Blood was flowing freely from her wrist down into a glass beaker. Umberto hadn't even detected the delicate aroma of the potent vitae for the stink of formaldehyde.

The rich red syrup wound its way through pipettes and tubing, now a liquid, now a cloud of ruddy vapor. At last, its essence dripped into the tub. It floated and swirled like a spiral of oil on the surface. As Sturbridge turned away to seal the wound, the trio of magicians completed their adjustments and the apparatus began to slurp up the mingled liquids and circulate them.

"If anything will bring him back, that will," Sturbridge said. "I will be back tomorrow to give it a fresh infusion. That pump needs to keep the preserving liquids circulating at all times. You understand? I will leave someone here to monitor the equipment if you would like, but it is largely unnecessary. As long as no one touches anything."

"I understand," Emmett replied hollowly, his eyes never straying from the still form at the center of the curious device. One edge of the sheet had worked itself loose and flapped idly in the turgid current. He hoped the sheet would not slip free entirely. "I thank you for coming, for what you have done."

"It is nothing," Sturbridge said. She laid a hand on Emmett's shoulder and he looked up. "I will find who did this, Emmett. Have no worry on that account. Now, are you all right?"

He shrugged and winced as the effort tore open the all-too-fresh wounds on his back. "I'll be fine," he said. "And we're out of tubs." When he smiled, he reveal twin rows of tusks scissoring wetly.

It was contagious. Sturbridge smiled in return. "Until tomorrow night then," she called, shooing her assistants ahead of her out of the chamber. "And Emmett, try to get some rest.

There's nothing more that you can do for him at this point that you haven't already done."

"Of course," he said. "Thank you again." But his eyes were lowered.

Already she knew that he would sit throughout the day in solitary vigil over his prince.

Chapter 22
De Veritatis

Three soft knocks at the door. The sound was faint, like the scratching of mice. Felton, seated at his desk, did not look up from his book. "Come in."

He heard the handle rattle, but the latch held. There was a brief pause and then the distinct clack as the latch was thrown open. Antigone stepped into the cell and resealed the door behind her.

"Good. For a moment there, I thought you had neglected to lock the door as we discussed. Good evening, Mr. Felton."

"You're late," he said. "Three nights late."

"You did not receive my message? I sent a note via one of the novices to tell you I would be unable to keep our appointment. Curious, she is usually one of the more reliable ones. Although admittedly this is largely due to the fact that she has spent the better part of the last two years trying to hack into the chantry's autonomic defense system and she doesn't want me to know about it."

He closed his book. The sound echoed like a gunshot in the tiny room. Picking up an envelope from the desk, he turned and raised it to where she could see it. "No need to discipline your messenger, I got the note all right. She slipped it under the door. But you still broke your promise. I'm not in a position right now where I can afford to trust a lot of people. And you're not making things any easier."

"Perhaps I should come back another time," she said.

"Don't you dare. Sit down." He gestured to the bed. "I'm going stir crazy in here and you think I'm going to let you just take off for another three nights leaving me in the dark about what's going on? What have you got for me? What are they saying out there? On the news? In the papers?"

Antigone perched on the edge of the bed. To Felton it looked as if any sudden move might startle her into flight. He turned his chair to face her. In the cramped quarters, their knees were nearly touching.

"One question at a time," she said. "You're going to run up quite a tab if you keep going at that rate."

He did not smile. "Okay, you got a cigarette?"

"Nope. Don't smoke. Not unless I'm set on… Never mind, it's an old joke. And probably not really that funny in the present circumstances. So, the news. The papers and the TV are all full of stories of arsonists and mad bombers. The police have leapt to an arrest, but it's not going to stick. It's already become one of those heads-will-roll embarrassments to the force. Some Palestinian group operating out of France is claiming credit for the attack, but that's even less credible. And the FBI guys are gearing up for a interstate manhunt. Oh yes, and you didn't kill the prince. I thought you might like to know that. You didn't really kill anyone, as far as I can determine. Well, no one other than a handful of gawkers who straggled into the fallout umbrella. But I think it would be safe to say that you did manage to really piss him off. I don't know the prince that well personally, do you think he's the type to hold a grudge?"

"I didn't blow up that building!"

"All right, I'll play along. Who did?"

Felton slammed a fist down on the desk. The books and papers jumped in unison. "Damn it, if I knew that, would I be here? I'm one of the victims here, remember? I was set up. I came to you for help."

"I'd like to help you, Mr. Felton. But you're going to have to be a bit more forthcoming. There are certain details of this case—surrounding your 'coincidentally' showing up at the Empire State Building at the exact time someone detonates a bomb on the observation deck—that somehow just don't sit right with me."

"I told you, I was... No, never mind. I thought that you could help me figure out who was behind all this. I thought, okay, even if the police and the FBI and the prince all struck out on this one, you guys would have some...means of finding out. They say there isn't anything that the Tremere can't come up with—if only you're willing to pay the price. So I figured maybe I could strike a deal. Maybe... Forget it. I'm wasting my time here. Doing nothing. Sitting around reading—who *is* this guy?" He checked the spine. "Thomas Aquinas, for Christsakes."

"*De Veritatis.*" Antigone smiled. "*On the Nature of Truth.* Your choice, or Brother Anselm's?"

"You think I read this kind of stuff for fun?" he shouted. "I—"

"Why are you reading it?" she asked in a quiet voice.

For a moment, she thought that he would hit her. He pushed his chair back violently and stood up, although there was not enough room behind him to do so gracefully. He ended up stumbling over her feet. Recovering, he began pacing the narrow stretch of floor between the desk and door, now more angry at himself than at her.

"I don't know. Just stupid, I guess. I thought if I played along, if I followed your stupid rules, if I pretended I wasn't in prison—then you guys might stick to your end of the bargain. You might believe me. You might help me track down the bomber and get myself out of this mess. Stupid. I should have known exactly how much you value your promises."

"Mr. Felton, I believe that I can help you, that we can help one another. I hope you will pardon my frankness, but I will point out to you that so far, in our relations, this house has been exclusively on the giving end. We have provided you sanctuary, we have taken you in, shielded you from the police and from the prince at no little risk to ourselves. We have taken steps to protect you from discovery by both mundane and arcane means. We have provided you with hospitality, sustenance and safe haven. And to date we have yet to receive anything in return. For the moment, I will be satisfied with some straight answers. Why were you at the Empire State Building that night?"

Felton dropped his head, unable to meet her gaze. When at last he spoke, it was barely in a whisper. "I was there to kill Emmett, the prince's right-hand man."

"Thank you, Mr. Felton. I believe you. Were you aware that the prince was also present when you set the bomb?"

He whirled upon her. "Are you even listening to me? I didn't set off any bomb! All I had on me was a pair of Uzis. It's all right here, if you don't believe me."

He stalked to the desk and took out a battered manila folder. Antigone recognized it instantly. It was the 'evidence' he had asked her to save for him during their previous meeting.

He brandished the file at her until she accepted it and peered inside. She took her time reading the documents as he glowered over her shoulder. She was only skimming, but had no wish to convey the impression that she had already perused the contents of the folder in some detail. She had, after all, given him her assurances that no one would read his papers.

Antigone had been as honest as the situation permitted. She had not actually had any intention of reading Felton's papers until after he had insisted upon saving them. Then, of course, it was her duty to 'clear' them. It was only a half-truth. In her line of work, you couldn't sit around fretting over the half-truths.

After all, she had also told him that he wasn't a prisoner. She wasn't sure that was even a half-truth.

"This is very illuminating. I am only saddened that you did not think fit to confide in me earlier. Now, can you tell me who assigned you this—" she glanced at the first page again— "mission Briefing?"

"No," he replied levelly. "That would put you at risk. Both of us, actually."

"Then I don't see how I can possibly—"

"Look. I don't know what would happen if I tried to betray the secrets of the..." The word *Conventicle* was on his lips, but he feared to give away even that much. "Of the group. I don't know what kind of compulsion I may have been placed under when I was initiated. But there was some kind of rite. A *blood rite*."

"I understand," she said. It was not merely a platitude. She had a first-hand knowledge of exactly what was involved in those rites. "We can have someone check that out. A blood rite leaves certain signatures that will give us some pretty good clues as to the nature of the binding and what it might take to break it. Please, go on."

"Well, let's just say that if it turns out that these guys were involved in me getting set up, all bets are off. I'm going to do whatever I have to do to bring them down."

"That's another one of those dangerous open-ended promises, Mr. Felton. You really should be more careful. But it will suffice. If your 'group' is not involved in this, then there is really no reason for me to know anything more about them, now is there?"

He grunted. "Then you think you can help? You think there's really some way of discovering who set the bomb?"

"Of course there is, Mr. Felton. There are any number of ways. The real trick for us is in determining which ways will prove more effective than the methods employed by the police, the FBI and the prince thus far. Fortunately, I also have spent some time in research over the past few nights and I think I may have a solution."

Retaking his seat, he leaned forward, elbows on knees. His face was pressed almost right up against her own. "I'm all ears."

"Unfortunately, the method may prove a bit risky. You're not adverse to a bit of danger, are you, Mr. Felton?"

"We have already established that I spend much of my recreational time killing people."

"Excellent. There is a simple rite that might serve our purpose, but to enact it, we will have to return to the scene of the crime."

"You're joking. That place is going to be crawling with cops. And the agents of the prince. None of these folks is going to be real understanding about me waltzing back in there for a midnight stroll along the observation deck. I mean—"

"Are you willing to do it, or aren't you?" she demanded.

"What are my other options?"

"You can go back to the Aquinas until we can come up with something else."

"How long might that be? Never mind. We'll do it. We'll just do it. Have you got any thoughts as to how we might get to the observation deck? I thought I saw something on the news about the elevator being blown up."

"I do. But it involves some thaumaturgy. So does the rite we need to perform on the observation deck. Did I mention that already?"

"No, but you didn't really have to. I don't suppose you can go through this little ritual without my being there?"

"Well, not without your blood…" Antigone replied.

"I thought you might say something like that. All right. I'm game. When do we go?"

"Tonight. Midnight. That *is* the best time for a midnight stroll."

"Great. Do I need to bring anything?" he asked resignedly.

"Nothing you would be likely to leave behind anyway. A few pints. I'm sure you'll do fine. I'll come for you here about 11:30. In the meanwhile, I've got a few preparations to see to."

"It's a date. You need any help getting things ready? I don't know spit about this human sacrifice stuff, but I can pack a bag and run through an equipment checklist."

"No, but thank you. Relax, Mr. Felton. You will need to conserve your strength."

As she turned to go, a thought struck him and he stopped her. "Ms. Baines, how does this little field trip affect our contract? I mean, you told me that I would have sanctuary as long as I remained within these walls...."

"An excellent point," she smiled. "It voids our agreement. There will be no guarantee that the chantry will take you back once you have left our protection. Are you still prepared to go through with this?"

Felton didn't have to think about it too long. It seemed that even when one caught the Tremere red-handed in wriggling through the little loopholes that riddled their agreements, there was really nothing you could do about it. "I don't have any choice, do I?"

"You always have choices, Mr. Felton. However, in this particular instance, you have exhausted your supply of better choices."

"I will see you tonight then," Felton said.

"Until tonight. Enjoy the Great Doctor." She tapped the heavy volume of Aquinas and let herself out. *"De Veritatis."* Smiling and shaking her head, she withdrew.

Chapter 23
Occam's Razor

Antigone emerged into a biting wind. Broken glass crunched underfoot. The observation deck of the Empire State Building was a blackened ruin, a landscape rendered in shredded chain-link fence and exposed concrete rebar. She walked to the very edge of the precipice and peered over. Below, she could see the twisted remains of the fiberglass catch-platforms piled high with rubble. They were not really intended to intercept anything more substantial than the inevitable coins pitched (either in curiosity or out of malice) over the parapet. If Emmett were to be believed, they had also saved the prince from plunging to his death. They looked decidedly worse for the wear.

Behind her, Felton stepped through the portal and gasped. As she turned, he was already moving forward, arms outstretched as if to snatch her back from the edge.

"For God's sake, hold still," he said skidding to a stop and nearly losing his own balance.

"And give you a stationary target? No, thank you, Mr. Felton." But she did step away from the ledge. "What were you doing, taking a running start at the portal?"

Felton lowered his gaze. "I jumped through. It seemed like the thing to do. At the time."

She smiled. "I see. Well, there's no need to be so hangdog about it. There's no real harm in it. That is, unless we had come out a few feet closer to the precipice. In future, though, you can just step through. The important thing is to do it boldly, unflinchingly. Some novices hesitate in the middle of their first apportation and get Waylaid. Held up in transit. I can remember one case of a novice not showing up at the destination until a week later. If that's not embarrassing enough, it bottlenecks the portal so no one else can use it." Then a thought occurred to her. "Master Ynnis didn't tell you to jump, did he?"

Felton shook his head, still embarrassed.

"Well, you didn't yell *Geronimo!*, at least. Did you?"

That got a smile out of him. "They don't yell *Geronimo!* anymore."

"They don't? Then what do they...oh, never mind. You'll do just fine on the way back."

"The way back?" he turned, a look close to panic on his face. "How the hell do we get back?" He stopped abruptly. On the ground behind him, a perfect circle had been swept clear in the midst of the broken glass and debris. Around its edge, shards of glass glittered in the form of tiny and precise glyphs. "How did—?"

She placed a reassuring hand upon his shoulder. "Between you and me? I have absolutely no idea. Master Ynnis is a wonder. He can do things with apportations that other folks haven't even thought up yet. They say he's got a special affinity for it. Because of his own precarious..."

She was about to say, "Because of his own precarious position upon the threshold." It was no secret that Master Ynnis had been Embraced at death's door. If he had not been hastily introduced into the company of the undying, he would certainly have been dead of a heart attack within a day or two at the outside. Although he had narrowly avoided the fatal coronary on that occasion, he had been forced to relive the moment dozens of times. The Embrace captured the body exactly as it was. That is how some Kindred (like herself) could still appear young, even after decades. Even such cosmetic details as the length of the hair or fingernails were fixed at the time of Embrace. No one really talked about the darker side of this operation. The fact was that all of a body's infirmities were captured as well, frozen, rendered perpetual. Master Ynnis was embraced at the threshold of a fatal cardiac arrest—a fate he was forced to suffer time and time again.

A heart attack could no longer kill him, of course. The source of his unnatural longevity lay elsewhere, beyond reach. But the confrontation with Helena was not the first time that Antigone had seen the ancient master totally incapacitated after strenuous exertion.

Antigone, however, remembered herself and who she was talking to. She decided to keep these thoughts to herself. The present situation required that she work very closely with Felton, at least until she had ascertained what part he had played in this bombing. But he was still an outsider. Even if, (as unlikely as it might be), he were proved innocent of all wrongdoing here, he was still an outsider.

"Because of his own precarious what?" Felton asked uncomprehendingly.

"Never mind, it will be okay. He'll hold the portal open for us. But I think we'll have more luck on the leeward side of the building, don't you?"

"If that means getting out of this wind, I'm all for it," Felton said. They walked around until the building shielded them from the worst of the wind. Felton stuck close to the shadow of the wall. Antigone, long skirts whipping, picked her way along the edge.

Absorbed in their exchange, neither Antigone nor Felton saw the shadowy figure that emerged from the diagram behind them. It kept very still, watching them from the shadow of the service elevator.

"I wish you wouldn't fool around near that ledge," Felton called.

"The height doesn't bother you, does it, Mr. Felton?"

He rolled his eyes. "Nope. But exposing myself to observation and sniper fire bothers me."

She stopped and peered around, scanning the sky, the streets below her, the windows of the surrounding buildings. "Point well taken." She returned toward the center of the walkway.

They rounded a corner and were suddenly free of the buffeting wind. "That's better. Shall we begin?"

"How do we start?" he replied.

"Well, you can start by clearing us a place to sit down. A rough circle would do."

He set about removing the larger pieces of debris and then scraping the broken glass out of the way with the side of his foot. "Will this do?"

"Excellent. Please be seated," she said. He put his back against the wall, his legs crossed in front of him. She sat facing him in some weird martial-artsy position—sitting back upon her right leg with her left folded up in front of her, knee pressed to her chest. "Are you ready?"

He nodded and she retrieved two objects from the pockets of her robes. One of them gleamed in the moonlight. "You ever strop one of these?" she asked, unfolding the wicked-looking straight razor.

"I'm good with knives," he said. "I'll give it a shot." He took the razor first, carefully, respectfully. And only then did he reach for the leather strop. He worked the blade up and down in long, confident strokes, honing its edge.

The oversized razor was very old and dulled. Rust dotted the ancient blade. It could have used a good whetstone and a professional sharpening, but Felton made do as best he could. He felt the blade warming to his touch. Despite its flaws, the razor felt good in his hand. It had a heft to it, a weight of history about it. The blade had obviously not spent all of its career whisker-fighting.

After a few unhurried minutes, he held the edge up to the light and examined it critically. He nodded once, satisfied. "It's not perfect, but that's good enough for a trench-water shave."

She regarded him with the same scrutiny he had previously turned on the ancient razor. "You ever shave in a trench, Mr. Felton?"

"Before my time," he shook his head. "It's all the same thing though. Hunkered down in a foxhole, a tunnel, a paddy. But they don't issue old timers like these anymore. Now you get a Bic razor—plastic, disposable—and you're happy to get that."

"A plastic razor. Can you cut yourself with a plastic razor? Your arm please." She held out her hand expectantly. Without hesitation, he complied. His right wrist settled into the palm of her hand.

"Not your wrists, if that's what you're thinking," he said. "Maybe that's what they were thinking, too. The quartermasters. Just keep talking so I don't know when it's coming, okay?"

She smiled. "Very well, listen to me very carefully then, Mr. Felton." With each word, she drew the blade farther down his forearm toward her. Very slowly. He winced with the sudden ice-hot pain, but held her eyes. She was opening him long and deep, tracing the line of blue vein all the way from elbow to wrist. "This is going to hurt a little bit. Please try not to scream. We do not want to attract undue attention. You're doing fine."

A harsh barking sound escaped his throat. It might have been a laugh.

"That's perfect," she said. "You are going to feel a bit lightheaded. That's perfectly normal. I want you to concentrate on the sound of my voice. Do you understand? There will be a rushing darkness in the periphery. There may be a sound there, like a train in the distance or a fluttering of dark wings. But I want you to ignore it and stay focused on my voice." His pupils dilated, his eyes darting restlessly from side to side.

"I said focus, mister! We're not losing anybody on my watch. Now, look at me. Look at me! You're going to be all right. This is just shock. You know about shock, right, soldier?"

"Blankets," he mumbled. "Elevate feet."

"That's right. Only we don't have time for all that right now, so we're going to do this thing fast. You ready? You've got to be ready. Now, listen. I'm going to count to three. When I do, I want you to look down at your arm. Do you understand? Good. Here we go. One, two, three."

As if of its own accord, Felton's head fell forward. He stared at his exposed arm, still clutched in her strong grip. The soft underside of his forearm was pristine, uncut.

"I...I don't understand."

"It is not necessary that you understand. You asked for a solution to help ferret out the bomber. A thaumaturgical solution." She folded the knife shut with one hand and laid it between them. "You don't want to turn back at this point, do you?"

"No," he said. "Go on."

"All right. Are you comfortable now?"

"Yes, I'm fine. Go right ahead."

Even as he pronounced the words, he felt the sharp pain again racing like fire the length of his forearm. He looked down to see a slight trickle of blood welling up on the surface of the skin and sliding away around the side of his arm.

He tried to jerk his hand away, but she kept her grip. She leaned in close and bore down harder upon his wrist. "Did you plant that bomb?" she demanded.

"No, I already told you all this. I was set up!" The trickle of blood had coagulated and ceased entirely.

"Then why were you here?"

"To kill Emmett. Why do we need to go over this again? Is someone else here? Listening to us?" He made as if to rise. She held him fast with her grip and glanced down at his forearm. Still nothing.

"How were you going to kill Emmett?"

"I was going to shoot him on his way in or out of the building. I didn't much care which. I had a mechanical triggering device, to let me know when the door opened. What's with the third degree all of a sudden?"

"Mr. Felton, who gave you this mission?"

"I thought we decided it was best that you not know the answer to that question," he replied.

"What was written upon the bone you pulled from the Bonespeaker's sackcloth?"

At this, his already shaken composure threatened to crack altogether. "How the hell..." he began and then with visible effort forced himself to calm down. "How the hell am I supposed to answer that?" he recovered. "What's a bonespeeder?"

"I said, 'Bonespeaker,' Mr. Felton. You need not act so surprised. We know a great deal about your little cabal. About your Rite of Drawing Down the Dragon. I cannot help you if you refuse to answer my questions. Now then, I asked you what was written on the bone?"

"Even if I knew what you were talking about, I don't see what possible difference something like that could make to you—"

"Tell me!" she barked directly into his face.

"A soap," he answered, the words leaping to his lips automatically before he could choke them off. "A white dragon."

He did not know how she had compelled him to speak against his will. He did not have the time to evaluate objectively what was happening to him. Nor did he have the opportunity to congratulate himself on his single irrevocable act of defiance. It was a credit to his years of training that the lie had instinctively reached his lips a fraction of a second before the truth.

The truth was drowned out beneath the animal howl of pain. As the lie crossed his lips, blood gushed from the gaping wound that sprung open, seemingly of its own accord, upon his forearm. The cruel cut stretched from elbow to wrist.

"That was very foolish, Mr. Felton. There is blood magic at work here, I have told you that already. Old magics and potent ones. Take this razor here, for instance. Can you feel the power in it? Its stroke falls, but the blood does not spill immediately. How can that be? Here, we will try again. What was written upon the bone?"

"South wind, damn you!" he rasped out. "Now let go of me. Let me bind this wound before I bleed to death."

"There is no need. You have already done so. The truth has amazing curative powers. I highly recommend it. Now, why did you lie and say you had drawn the dragon?"

He looked down and saw that it was exactly as she had said. The bleeding had abated, slowed to a trickle. Already he could see the clots forming and the pink flesh resealing itself. "I don't like this. I don't like this at all," he murmured to himself.

Antigone feared he was slipping deeper into shock. "Why?" she prompted.

"I don't know, I—" He felt a stab of pain from his forearm and cursed. "Give me a chance to think through it, would you?!"

She shrugged apologetically. "It's out of my hands now, Mr. Felton."

This pronouncement did not reassure him in the least. "All right! I lied because... It's a little hard to explain...."

"You lied because he teased you, belittled you. He called you 'hero.' He said you were afraid."

"No. I mean, sure he said those things, but that wasn't why. Geez, what do you take me for that you think he could play me like that?" Felton broke off uncertainly and fell silent.

"But somebody played you," Antigone said in a quiet voice. "You said that someone set you up."

"But he couldn't have known. That I would lie, I mean. Nothing like that's ever been done before. At least not as far as I know. Has it?" he finished somewhat lamely.

"Damn it, Felton, when you screw up, you screw up good. Of course the damned drawing can be fixed! How else could the Bonespeaker promise..."

"Promise what?" Felton pounced.

She shook her head. "Never mind. That's beside the point. You were telling me about why you lied."

"You've got a one-track mind, lady. And I get the feeling the train's not running my way. Look, I've played along with all this so far because you said you'd help me. But so far, all you've done is make demands and accusations. Now, I don't have to explain myself to you or anybody. My reasons are just personal and it's not something you would understand anyway."

"Try me," she said.

Felton regarded her for a long moment, as if to make sure he were replying of his own will and not in response to the tone of command in her voice. "I must be an idiot for even answering you. Look, you won't understand. You haven't been out there in the field as long as I have. Keeping up the good fight. Night after night. It's all I know. And damn it, I'm good at it. Everybody's got to be good at something, right? Well, this is what I do better than anybody else. I hunt down the Sabbat. I find out where they feed, where they carouse, where they go to ground in the morning.

"If I get a clean shot, I take one or two of them down. And I mark them, so the others will know who got them and so they'll be afraid. It gives us an edge the next night. It's nothing sicko or anything. Just a little trophy. I don't even keep them, I just throw them down the sewer or in a dumpster or whatever is nearby. But, damn it, going out on operations against the Sabbat is something I'm good at it. And it's all I know. And damn, it's hard to give it up and just be anybody again. I'm not going to be just anybody again."

His gaze was fierce and imploring. Antigone nodded. "I believe I can relate to that sentiment, Mr. Felton. For what it's worth, I believe you. You have passed the Test of the Razor. To tell you the truth, I was more than half hoping you would fail. It would have made things so much easier."

A shiver traveled the length of his spine. In that instant, he knew with certainty that, had things gone differently, she would have killed him without compunction. Or allowed him to bleed to death, which amounted to much the same thing. "So that's it? Now you know who set me up? The razor told you?"

"No, Mr. Felton. You told me. There is power in the blade, certainly. An old power, a power of names. It inherits its own name from a fourteenth-century Franciscan monk, William of Occam. Are you familiar with the principle of Occam's Razor?"

Felton heaved an exaggerated sigh, remembering the mountain of books on his desk back at the chantry. "Yes, I seem to recall reading something of that sort. Something about given two theories that explain all the facts, the simpler one is the better. But I thought that was only a rhetorical test—fit only for philosophers and orators—not some actual blade."

"Ideas can be invested with physical form, Mr. Felton. But the price is high and the results not always satisfactory. This blade is just such an actualized ideal, forged to cleave truth from falsehood. I am impressed. I did not know you were a scholar as well as a soldier."

"Well nobody's ever called me that before—not and walked away from it, anyway. It's no credit to me, though. Your Brother Anselm has been very thorough. Occam's Razor, Aquinas's *De Veritatis*, Diogenes's Lantern. Is this your standard reading list for the condemned?"

"You were not condemned, Mr. Felton. You were awaiting trial. And it cannot hurt a man awaiting trial to be fortified with truth. But the ordeal is behind you now and you have come through the fire relatively unscathed. I must remember to congratulate Brother Anselm on his excellent curriculum."

"I'm not sure you should encourage him. The boy already has clear ambitions of academic tyranny."

Antigone smiled. "It's gone beyond ambition, I'm afraid. The 'boy,' as you call him, is already over one hundred years old. He has been at the chantry for longer than I have."

"A hundred years. And he's made it all the way to assistant babysitter." Felton shook his head. "Boy, am I glad I wasn't embraced into Clan Tremere. What a petty, bureaucratic nightmare. No offense. It's just that sitting around for decades waiting my turn to get to be assistant junior nobody (second-class) just doesn't appeal to me."

She watched him for a while, taking her time in answering. "So you hook up with some outfit like the Conventicle. You put your ass on the line for them every night and for what? At the end of a decade or two or ten, what does it get you? No, I know what it gets you. Dead, just dead. You know of anybody who's been at that racket for longer than you, Felton? More than a decade or so?"

He shook his head. "Old Charlie might have a decade in. He hasn't been at it as long as I have, though. Shit, I don't think there's anybody around anymore who's been at it as long as I have."

"So you're calling all the shots now, right? You're the Bonespeaker, the head honcho. You tell folks where to go and what to do. Like all those assistant junior nobodies (second class) out there getting butchered in the streets every night, right?"

"Go to hell. I'm good at what I do. And it's what I want. You think I'd be happy keeping up with all the administrative b.s. of running the unit? Or officiating at all the stupid ceremonies, prancing around in some Halloween mask and cowl? Not me, thanks."

"No, I can't see you doing that. And if they all got together and forced you to be the boss, you know what you'd find? That the Bonespeaker was never really the guy calling the shots. That there was another level to the organization, someone who oversaw a handful of individual cells. And that you were still taking orders. That you had made it all the way to assistant junior nobody (first class). With the Tremere, at least, you know what you're getting into. Novices, regents, lords, pontifices, councilors. A clear chain of command. You always know exactly where you stand, even if you're not too happy about the footing."

"How many folks you know who ever made it to regent?" Felton asked.

"One," she replied levelly.

"One in what, twenty years? As close as I can figure it, you've got to have at least twenty years of service under your belt. How many times have you been promoted? You personally, I mean?

She did not bother to correct his math. "I am the acting head of security for the chantry," she replied coldly.

"All right, don't go getting pissed off now. I'm just trying to make a point. What does 'acting head of security' mean? Is that like a regent? Does that put you any closer to calling the shots? You don't wear the chevrons—the colors here or here or here like you told me to look for." He indicated her cuffs, collar and rope belt. "Does that mean you're beyond all that now? Or does it mean that 'acting head of security' doesn't carry any real muscle? That they haven't even bothered to promote you after twenty years of service?"

"Rank is not simply a function of length of service," she replied. She was not pleased with the hollow sound of the formulaic response on her lips. She had heard these words cited many times before and always in unpleasant circumstances. "There are...other considerations."

"Yeah, aren't there always," he said. "Look, all I'm saying is that we're not that different, you and I. We are the workhorses, the hard bodies that the machine runs on, feeds on. It doesn't really matter who's calling the shots. The bosses are all interchangeable. Regent, prince, Bonespeaker, it doesn't really matter which one you serve, which one you're bound to. It's all the same from where we're standing. Hell, I'm not sure I'd even notice if somebody suddenly pulled a switch and put the prince in charge of the chantry and the Bonespeaker in charge of the city and the regent in charge of the Conventicle. I've still got to get up and do the same thing I've done every night. It's what I know."

Her look was distant and his words didn't seem to register upon her. "I think it time that we headed back now, Mr. Felton. Under the current circumstance, I cannot see any reason that we should deny you reentry into the protection of the chantry. You may reclaim your right of sanctuary and it will be as if you had never ventured forth."

"Thanks," he said, realizing just how close he had come to being abandoned to his own fate here on the wind-swept precipice. He had not considered that Antigone might use the portal to return, only to seal it behind her. He had a momentary vision of that exile. Perhaps he could have hidden from the deadly rays of the sun in the recess of the destroyed elevator shaft. He might have survived several days and nights of this captivity, until the hunger became unbearable. Then there was no telling what desperate (and possibly suicidal) measures he might be forced to, once the ravenous Beast had achieved the upper hand.

They walked around the building in silence until they again came to the portal. He looked at her nervously.

"You go through first," she said. "You can just step through this time. I will follow you shortly. There are things I must attend to." When he gave her a questioning look, she explained further. "I would clear away all signs that we have been here."

That seemed to satisfy him, but still he did not step into the circle. "I'd rather know the worst now," he said. "You told me earlier that you knew who set me up."

"I do. You told me yourself. I only needed to verify that you were telling me the truth. About the details of the hit, and about how you got drawn into it. Occam's Razor has corroborated your story. You are cleared of all wrongdoing, in my mind at least. The prince and the mortal authorities will not be so easy to convince."

"Then who planted that bomb? Who set me up?"

"No one set you up, Mr. Felton. Or, to put it more accurately, you set yourself up. You have admitted as much. That dragon was never intended for you. No one could have known that you would, capriciously and deliberately, derail the rite and claim the mission for your own."

"But...but it doesn't add up. *Somebody* was set up, I know that. You're not about to brush that aside or change my mind on that point. I was there. I know a set-up when I waltz into one."

"You do this often, then? No, never mind. All right, let's say it was a set-up. Let's say *someone* was intended to draw that dragon. Maybe it didn't matter who, as long as somebody was there when the bomb went off. To take the heat and divert attention from the real culprit. In your professional opinion, Mr. Felton, is that scenario in keeping with your impressions—at the rite and then at the scene of the crime?"

"Thank you, Ms. Baines. It's reassuring to think I have worked this hard only to become an 'expert' on betrayals and crime scenes. But you're right. The whole thing could have been engineered so that one of us—of the Conventicle, I mean—would take the fall."

"Can you remember who precisely placed the idea for that hit before the group?"

"You do know an awful lot about our inner workings, don't you? I can't put my finger on who in particular that was. But it shouldn't really matter. A petitioner doesn't have any direct control over when or where a mission will be carried out. The only one who could influence that is the person who writes the briefing."

"That's already been checked out," Antigone replied promptly. Let him wonder about what kind of thaumaturgical signatures she could pick up and trace back to their creator simply by perusing the manila folder in question. She did not feel it necessary to mention that it was she who had assembled that dossier. "No help there. And the timing of the hit would still be problematic. The person writing the briefing would have no control over the exact time the mission would be carried out. That would be determined by the date of the meeting and the time the hitman was released from the room."

"It's hopeless," Felton said. "Too many questions and nobody to beat an answer out of. As much as it goes against my best judgment, it may be time I dropped in on my old friends again."

"I think you may be right. But you're not going back there alone. Is there anyone else on the inside that we can rely upon?"

"We? Who said anything about we?" Felton demanded. "They see me coming with some stranger in tow and it's all over. Neither one of us would get any further than the more private side of the front door. Where there wouldn't be any chance witnesses."

"I don't think my presence would cause quite the uproar you are envisioning. But we will arrive separately just to be sure. I should already be in place when you arrive, in case there is trouble. And your friend…?"

Felton shook his head. "Charlie," he supplied. "Damn, is there anything about all this you don't know? He's the only one I've seen since…since everything went crazy. He gave me the number in case I needed somebody to bust me out of here." He laughed.

"Yes, Charlie. We will want to get him in on this as well. So long as you think he can be relied upon. At this point, we can use all the help we can get."

"If it's all the same to you," he said. "I think I'd rather leave Charlie out of it. Not that he can't be trusted or anything. It's just that…well, he's doing all right for himself now. For a change. He's got his own place and a little business on the side, even a family…of sorts. He doesn't need to go getting mixed up in something like this. Any further than he already is. I don't want him throwing it all away on my account."

She regarded him curiously, but said nothing.

"Well, I guess that's settled then. I'll see you back at the old jail." He squared himself to the circle and took a deep breath. "Here goes nothing. And Ms. Baines…thanks."

"No, thank you, Mr. Felton. Try to get some rest."

He muttered something that sounded vaguely like "Geronimo!" and leapt into the circle with both feet.

Chapter 24
Credo

Antigone methodically paced off the circuit of the observation deck. Her footfalls stuck close to the very edge of the abyss. She veered aside from this precarious course only once, to pick her way clear of a pile of twisted debris, the remains of a chrome viewer. The dizzying height and the proximity of the raw and fatal edge steadied her. It was a comforting, familiar sort of peril. Far preferable to the uncertain dangers that lay ahead.

The sensation reminded her of youthful excursions out onto the forbidden widow's walk of her childhood home back in Scoville. The widow's walk was a kind of narrow porch ringing the upper reaches of the house on its seaward side. It could only be reached through a pair of French doors off the master bedroom on the uppermost floor. Many of the old homes along the coastline could boast such a morbid promontory. It was a place where the lady of the house could come at sundown and stare far out to sea—wondering if this would be the day that the ocean would bring her husband home to her.

As far back as Antigone could remember, the widow's walk had always been her mother's exclusive domain. It was a hard-won privilege and one she jealously guarded. She wore it like a badge of honor—the mark of a woman forced to the indignity of sharing her man with the fickle and capricious sea.

Of course there were any number of sound reasons for keeping little girls well clear of such places. Reasons that she and her mother knew only too well. Mother had been forced into the habit of keeping the doors locked against further misfortune. Losing a husband had nearly destroyed her (or destroyed all but a small part of her); losing one of her girls at this point might well finish the job.

Antigone could still remember the thrill of the first time she had sneaked the key from its curio box on the vanity. She could not have been more than six or seven. She could remember struggling with the lock, certain that her clumsy scrabblings would be overheard. Mother had gone into town but if Electra should discover Antigone here…

With a satisfying click, the key turned and she pushed the doors open a crack and peered through, as if the peril of discovery awaited her on the other side of the door instead of on this one. Feeling foolish and awkward and exposed, she edged out onto the walk.

A damp spring breeze was blowing off the water. It caught a trailing strand of her long hair and plastered it across the corner of her mouth. She smoothed it aside, fancying that she could almost taste the hint of salt and fish on the wind. She jumped at the sound of her own footfalls on the rough-hewn planks. Squeezing her eyes closed, she muttered a verse to herself that was said to be proof against prying eyes. Then she stepped boldly forward, reaching up to seize the railing in both fists. She peered through the bars, and the ocean, as if aware it were being watched, puffed out its chest and swelled to fill her view.

It was all-encompassing. Antigone felt as if she were being swallowed up in the vastness of that sea, losing herself. Her hair billowed out upon the waves like seaweed, reaching toward, but always coming up tantalizingly short of, the elusive horizon. There was no sense of panic or helplessness as there might be in the realization that you were drowning or falling.

Rather it was as if there were really two bodies of water (had always been two, she realized with sudden intensity). One was a vast sea, strong, complete and brim-filling the entire world. The other was small and confused and alone—its entirety stoppered up inside a single clay vessel and set adrift. From this position of confinement, Antigone had never once suspected the existence, much less the proximity, of her vast counterpart. Not until this chance encounter shattered the clay vessel and spilled her out into the ocean's arms. The two waters mingled and became indistinguishable.

Antigone did not know, nor could she later reconstruct, exactly how long she had lingered there, vast, strong and complete at last. Brim-filling the entire world. It was a small, delicate sound that brought her back to herself, back to the confines of the clay vessel of her six-year-old body. A discordant note.

Feeling loss and betrayal, she turned angrily toward the source of the sound. There, at the very corner where the widow's walk met the house, wedged between the wall and the first bar of the railing, was an untidy brown tangle. A bird's nest.

The very sight of it brought Antigone up short. Her footfalls became more guarded, stealthy. She crept forward and peered into the nest. Three eggs, robin blue. One of them was already cracked open and lying in two halves. Another was, even now, in the process of disgorging its contents. She could see the blunt, mucousy egg-tooth jerking and striking again and again.

The weak, incessant chirping that had disturbed her came from the hatchling that had already won its freedom. Its eyes were still closed. It could not see her and it did not turn toward her expectantly, anticipating food or comfort.

Growing bolder, she edged up very close to the nest, the tip of one shoe brushing right up against it. Carefully, deliberately, she worked the tip of that shoe slowly back and forth. With each movement, she gradually insinuated it further and further under the lip of the nest. The egg in the midst of hatching rolled over and she could no longer see its occupant's progress. That was some small relief.

It did not take as long as one might imagine—only a few moments really—for her toe to nestle its way under the very center of the tangle of twigs. Another pass and the whole unbalanced, teetering dangerously on the edge of the widow's walk before surrendering to the inevitable, to the long fall to the front yard.

Antigone didn't peer out over the edge to watch it fall, or even crane forward to listen for the crunch of broken twigs. She was busy kicking at the last few tenacious bits of the nest that still lodged up against the corner of the house.

Satisfied, she returned to the house without a further glance at the ocean. She carefully closed and locked the doors behind her and sealed the key back up in its curio box. Later that evening, she saw Medea playing in the living room with a broken blue-speckled eggshell.

Antigone scuffed at the nearest pile of debris with one toe, sending it cascading out into the abyss. Moments later she heard a soft pattering like rain falling upon the catch platform below.

Blackened ash and soot were pervasive. The best efforts of the wind had been unable to accomplish even something so basic as sweeping the deck clear. Antigone felt spent, used up. She had gone to the Conventicle…why? To prove herself. To be somewhere where her abilities and talents mattered. What hope of earning advancement—or even the respect of her brothers and sisters—did she have among the Tremere? After over seventy years of struggle, it had become painfully obvious to everyone around her that she had no aptitude for magic. Medea would have made a good thaumaturge, but Antigone? She was hopeless.

The very existence of the Pyramid was an act of magic, an angry credo hurled in the face of polite Kindred society. Its message was the same as that of the Great Pyramid at Giza: *I will endure.*

Beyond life, beyond death, *I will endure.* Despite all obstacles and opposition, *I will endure.* Born in ancient blood spilled in the Darkest Age; tempered in the fires of the Inquisition; proven in the forging of the crown of the Camarilla and the blood-fetter that had brought the rebellious clans to heel—*I will endure.*

The very design of the Great Pyramid was a magical diagram constructed to convey the pharaoh from this life to the next. The Tremere Pyramid had promised to be just such a portal for Antigone, easing her passage between lifetimes, the enticing escape trick she could never quite resist coming back for, again and again.

But instead of propelling her onward, the sacred geometry of the Tremere tomb had turned upon her, proving to be a labyrinth, a trap. Without any hope of attaining more than a rudimentary grasp of the secrets of thaumaturgy, she could not hope to move forward. She could certainly never go back. At times, she wished the Pyramid would just release her, turn her back out into the desert of the streets of New York. To fend for herself. To find her own way.

But that was not the way of the Pyramid. It endured. It never gave up. It never abandoned its own. These very strengths, however, were Antigone's bane. She was caught in stasis, cursed to wander the empty halls of the pyramid

208 / Eric Griffin

eternally. To protect the tomb's secrets from foolhardy grave robbers. To ward the restless dead all around her.

There was only one thing she could think of that could now release her from her bond of service to the Pyramid, from her oath to Clan Tremere, from her seventh (and perhaps final) lifetime.

The minotaur, at least, had his Theseus to look forward to. The hero's coming had been foretold. Surely they could not have kept something like that from the bull-headed young prince. He knew that there was a redemption at hand, a redemption in blood. Perhaps many years and the breadth of seas still lay between them, but there would be a redemption.

Antigone had no such assurance. If she were going to pass beyond this seventh lifetime, she would have to do it the old-fashioned way. She had worked the trick many times before. It was a humble magic—not of spilling blood and obsidian knives and chalk diagramma and candlelight—but of boldly walking the treacherous line, the fine edge where death and names met. Where the two mingled, dissolved and coalesced into something new.

She leaned far out over the abyss, rocking forward on the balls of her feet, trying to find the fulcrum, the exact still-point between standing upright and toppling outward and down. There.

She hung there, suspended between worlds. Utterly weightless. She was at the very crux. From here, something as simple as a gust of wind would suffice to send her plummeting end over end toward the waiting pavement below.

She inhaled deeply of the cool night air, savoring the undiluted freedom of it. One by one, she surrendered her thoughts to it, releasing them like delicate, fluttering birds. She watched as each of them in turn swooped, cut, spiraled outward. Into the anonymity of the night wind.

Antigone stood alone, empty of all thought, desire, will. A living thing no longer, but rather a mute witness, an extension of the parapet. A construct of night air and pure altitude.

Now even the strongest wind could not hope to dislodge her. The gusting breeze blew right through her without so much as ruffling her garments. Time itself seemed to fall away from her, spilling over the edge of the yawning precipice. Stretching away.

She would never be sure what exactly it was that called her back from that strange communion upon the brink. At first she thought it was merely some rustling of ash and broken glass behind her, stirred up by the wind's passing. Then she realized that the movement was not external to her at all. The wind had stirred something within her. And that something had stepped forward in answer to the wind's question and acted.

A decision had been made, a fundamental decision. By reducing herself to the essential, Antigone had stripped away all occluding barriers of confusion, desire, self-deceit. She had chosen to endure.

If this decision were a victory, however, it was a fleeting one. Even as she became aware of herself once more, Antigone seemed to deflate. She rocked back onto her heels, her entire form shrinking back away from the ledge. Collapsing in upon itself. She felt numb, a somnambulist. Dimly, she became aware of a nagging, surging, feeling of loss.

Resignedly, she turned her back on the city spread out below her and set her steps back toward home. Each step carried her closer to what had become, for her, the mundane. The chantry, the Tremere Pyramid, the trap of her nightly existence. Resignedly, she stepped over the threshold of the mystic *diagramma* and felt the first unsettling jolt of the apportation.

Absorbed in her own thoughts, Antigone never saw the shadowy form near the elevator shaft. A figure who seemed to follow her every movement with a strange mixture of curiosity and concern.

Chapter 25
Fire and the Stake

Antigone emerged from the diagramma into Master Ynnis's sanctum. The furnishings were minimal and utilitarian. Even when demonstrating his craft before a class of novices, it was Ynnis's practice to sit on the floor—the traditional canvas for the apportationist's art.

The two gentlemen present in the room when Antigone appeared were no students. They stood rigidly, looking slightly awkward and out of place. She had never seen either of them before. They both wore expensive dark suits of a continental cut—one achingly modern, the other fashionable just before the turn of the century. The nineteenth century.

The former stepped forward as she arrived and took her arm. "Miss Baines? I'm glad you're here. My name is Stephens, this is Mr. Himes. We're here on official business and we could really use your help. Do you mind if we ask you a few questions?"

He ushered her toward the door and his counterpart fell into step alongside them. Antigone dug in her heels and tried to extricate her arm from his grasp. "Where is Master Ynnis?" she demanded. "Where is Mr. Fel…"

Stephens exchanged glances with Himes. "Master Ynnis has gone on ahead to help get the novices settled down. Mr. Fell has been returned to his cell. That was a risky thing you did, Miss

Baines. Dangerous criminal like that. Someone could have been hurt. *You* could have been hurt. Is that standard security-team practice around here? Taking fugitives back to the scene of the crime?"

"Look, I don't know who the hell you are, but I don't like what you're playing at. I don't intend to be questioned and I don't intend to be manhandled. You've got about thirty seconds to convince me why I shouldn't just turn the chantry security system on you."

Himes cleared his throat. "That is actually one of the very things we would like to ask you about, ehm, Miss Baines. We will need your security codes. Now would be a good time, if it please you." He smiled, his eyes never lifting from the polished tips of his shoes. He seemed slightly embarrassed by the entire proceeding.

Antigone looked from one to the other. "You can't be serious."

"We are very serious, Miss Baines," Stephens pressed forward again, uncomfortably close.

"Look, how about we start all over again. You can start by telling me who you are and what the hell you're doing here. And I cannot advise your trying to take my arm again, Mr. Stephens. I have already made my feelings on this matter quite clear, and the autonomic defensive systems will construe any renewed familiarity on your part as an assault. It is authorized to use disabling force in such situations."

"Perhaps my partner was a bit abrupt, Miss Baines," Himes stammered. "I don't believe he has made himself clear. We are here on official business. From Vienna."

It was clear that this latest pronouncement had gotten through. Antigone looked as if the wind had been knocked out of her. She took a half step backward to steady herself. "No, you can't be," she muttered absently. "You are the Ast...?"

"We are special operatives," Himes said. "From the Fatherhouse. The news that has reached us of late has been, hmm, somewhat disturbing. We had hoped that you might help us clear up any misunderstanding. Your cooperation in this matter would, how do you say, would not go unnoted." He smiled up at her and offered his arm.

Antigone tried to think, but all that kept racing through her mind were horror stories about the 'liquidation' in Tel Aviv. She tried to picture this mumbling, unassuming old man purging the chantry house, wielding fire and the stake. It was jarring, almost preposterous.

"I…I don't know. I don't know what help I could be, I mean. I'm just a novice."

Just a novice. Her own words were bitter in her mouth. These gentlemen—these *Astors*, she corrected herself—knew exactly what she was. They probably even knew exactly how long she would remain that way. Antigone found herself quickly sizing up her chances here. She didn't like her odds.

Himes smiled at her, a nervous smile trying to be brave, one you might use to coax someone down from a ledge. "It's all right, Miss Baines. It's just a few questions. I think you can be a great help to us if you will only try. You will try, won't you?"

Antigone felt the noose tightening around her. She glanced nervously from one man to the other.

"Of course she will," Stephens said, all smooth confidence. He dismissed any lingering uncertainties with a wave of his hand. "Miss Baines here is a smart cookie. She knows how to look after herself. Yes sir, she's gonna come through this just fine. All she has to do is what she would do normally. She's a chantry security officer. She sees things. When she sees a problem, something out of the ordinary, something that disturbs her, she reports it. That's how she keeps things running smoothly around here. Isn't that right, Antigone? May I call you Antigone?

She recoiled. Her name sent shivers up her back.

Taking her silence as consent, he pressed on. "Antigone, you know what's been going on here. Murders, bombings, assassinations. It's madness. All of this has to stop. All of this *will* stop. We're here to make sure of it. All I'm asking for is your help, all right? Where is the ambassador?"

Antigone spoke, the words leaping to her lips almost without her volition. Her voice sounded hollow and empty. "Dead. In the crypts. At the bottom of the well."

"You see!" He turned a triumphant look upon Himes. "I told you she would do the right thing. She's one of the smart ones. She's going to come out of this just fine. Now, Antigone, tell me, how did he die?"

It was as if she were watching herself from over her own shoulder. She saw her simulacrum's mouth moving in synch with the puppeteer's hand motions. "He fell. From a ledge. It is...not safe down there."

Stephens nodded to Himes before turning back to her with his most winning smile. "You're doing great. Now tell me, why was he down in these crypts?"

Antigone wanted to shout at the pathetic little ventriloquist's dummy that had been so carefully crafted in her own image. She wanted to smash it. To make it stop. "He and Eva and Sturbridge went down there together. And now he's dead. And Eva's dead. And Sturbridge is—" She broke off.

"Yes? What about Regent Sturbridge?" he coaxed.

"I'm afraid," she said. "I'm afraid that she can't keep it all down. It was foolish to try to swallow them all. The nightmare is bigger than she is. Far greater. She should have known that. She should never have..."

"There, there. It's all right," Stephens caught Himes's eye and gave a subtle hand signal. Himes slowly began moving in on the near-hysterical novice while Stephens kept up a steady, soothing monologue. "Sturbridge is going to be fine. We can get her the help she needs. We just need to know where to find her. Do you know where Regent Sturbridge is, Antigone?"

He laid a hand reassuringly on her arm.

All hell broke loose. There was a sharp retort and the unmistakable reek of ozone filled the tiny sanctum. Stephens yanked back his hand with a howl of pain, cradling the seared fist to his chest. Antigone could see that his sleeve still smoldered from where the autonomic defense system had targeted him. Himes, startled by the blast, lunged toward her and then immediately thought better of it, catching himself before he suffered a similar fate.

The force of the blow broke the strange dislocation that Stephens's words had cast over her. Antigone found herself, for better or worse, once again firmly within her own body. Her first thought was to flee. Taking advantage of the momentary confusion, she leapt toward the *diagramma hermetica* and vanished across its threshold.

Chapter 26
The Widow's Walk

Antigone landed heavily and skidded toward the edge of the rooftop. She teetered precariously upon its edge, her arms flailing for balance. She knew an uncharacteristic moment of panic. Apparently that same part of her that had, a short while before, decided that it would endure was reluctant to have this decision summarily reversed.

She caught her balance and turned, half in panic, expecting signs of pursuit. The circle of artfully arranged glass shards was empty. There was still time.

With one foot, she swiped angrily at the diagram, sweeping a wide swath from the pattern. That ought to keep anyone from following her through.

Then a more disturbing thought occurred to her. A determined pursuer might not be frustrated by the closing of this one means of ingress. She had reason to believe that the Astors were nothing if not determined. If this doorway were closed to them, they might open another.

Swiftly, Antigone stooped and began methodically rearranging the delicate glass mosaic—repairing the damage she had done here, subtly altering a supporting glyph there. She was working from memory, reconstructing a pattern she had only briefly glimpsed in the crypts below the Chantry of Five

Boroughs. And even she had to admit, it was a pattern she only imperfectly understood. A protective circle, inverted.

She was still bent over the carefully arranged slivers of glass—trying to recall the correct conjugation of the rune of elemental warding—when Stephens stepped through. Antigone threw up her arms defensively and nearly tumbled over backward.

Stephens's momentum carried him forward and he forcibly rebounded from the outer ring of wardings. His features contorted as if he had run full out into an invisible pane of glass.

He towered over her, mouthing silent words, entreaties, threats, but no sound penetrated the barrier. Antigone sat down heavily, her arms out behind her to catch her fall. She could feel the cruel shards of glass penetrating her palms, but still she could not tear herself away from the demand in his eyes. It held her there, pinned, wriggling, under glass. She could neither move nor speak beneath the weight of his expectation.

"Brava!"

The voice, directly behind her, startled her out of this fascination. Antigone braced herself for a new attack from an unexpected corner. Very carefully, she brushed her hands upon the front of her robes, dislodging a gentle rain of glass slivers. Gathering what dignity she could muster she straightened regally and turned to face this new threat.

"You!" she accused. "How long have you been—"

"Easy, little one," Sturbridge replied, coming forward out of the shadow of the service elevator. "Long enough. I saw your razor's rite earlier, and now this. Very impressive. Quite innovative."

Sturbridge circled the diagram, the prisoner's eyes following her every move. She pointedly ignored him. "May I?" she asked Antigone.

Not really knowing what to expect, Antigone nodded mute agreement. Sturbridge bent and rearranged one of the

218 / Eric Griffin

supporting glyphs, muttering under her breath the entire time. Antigone caught a snatch of what seemed a chant in a harsh, guttural tongue.

Suddenly, the tiny pinpricks of moonlight reflected in each shard of glass caught life and flared blindingly. Squinting through the blaze, Antigone saw Stephens's visage contort in a howl of pain and frustration. An instant later, it vanished entirely.

Smiling, Sturbridge turned to Antigone. In spite of herself, concern was apparent in the novice's unguarded features. "He's not...?"

"No, he'll be fine. I've just taken him out of harm's way for a little while. That particular confinement diagram is not an overly pleasant one. There's a perfectly good reason that the Convention banned its use back in the fifteenth century. Incidentally, I might mention that you are now officially under censure for the invoking a *verboten* dark thaumaturgic rite. Still, it was very neatly done, and pulled off under duress, I might add. Quite remarkable. I would be inclined toward leniency, but the gentleman in question would be well within his rights to insist upon the full penalty prescribed by the law. By rights you should burn for it. A friend of yours?"

Antigone's mouth hung open. She tried to protest. "But, Regentia! I didn't know... I didn't mean to... Oh, Regentia, he is an Astor!"

Sturbridge accepted this new assertion without challenge. "Hmm. That does rather complicate things. These Astors tend to be very letter-of-the-law. I don't suppose he has any compelling reason for wanting you alive?"

"He...they wanted to ask me a bunch of questions. About the ambassador and about Eva and about you. That and they wanted my security codes."

Sturbridge looked disappointed. "Not quite the skeleton in the closet we're looking for here, I'm afraid. I don't know if we even have a proper burning stake anymore. Well, if they're going to condemn you for this, we can at least make sure they can't just hush it up. They may close down the chantry by tomorrow night, but that leaves us an evening to set right what we may. Please kneel."

"Regentia?"

Sturbridge, not waiting upon the assumed compliance, closed her eyes and began to recite in a dead tongue. Her voice had the hint of reverence usually reserved for scripture or poetry. Flustered, Antigone hurriedly knelt before Sturbridge, hoping her superior had not noticed her hesitation. Her features were composed, resigned. Her head bowed as before the axe of judgment.

Sturbridge reached out a hand expectantly, palm upward. Steeling herself, Antigone placed her hand within the regent's and braced herself against the inevitable blow. She felt the firm pressure of Sturbridge's touch, but there was no warmth in it. The flesh felt piscine — rough, chill, damp. It reminded her of the brush of pudgy bluish fingers from a recurring nightmare.

Antigone promised herself she would not flinch away. The slightest of whimpers escaped her lips as she felt flesh part, and she immediately berated herself for her show of weakness before her regent. Her eyes burned with shame and she felt the warm flush of vitae surging down her arm, over the hump of her wrist, streaming between her fingers in long, viscous tendrils. She kept her eyes pressed tightly shut and stifled a betraying sob.

Sturbridge was speaking again, that same guttural monotone, but Antigone could no longer pick out the words, much less their meaning. Something hot and wet splashed against the side of her face and she recoiled, twisting away from the point of impact. Almost against her will, her eyes flew open, only to see the next blow already descending.

Sturbridge's cupped hand slashed downward again. The blow fell this time upon Antigone's right side—the fistful of her own vitae broke upon her collarbone like a wave. Its hot spume washed up and over her jawline, a mirror image of the previous blow.

Uncomprehendingly, Antigone gazed up at Sturbridge as if she saw, not her familiar regent, but some macabre avenging angel. In Sturbridge's eyes, however, Antigone saw no trace of malice, no trace of righteous retribution, of justice served. There was only solemnity, and a strange hint of pride.

Antigone could not hold her regent's gaze. Confused and frightened she cast her head downward. Her attention was captured by the two angry red weals—painted, she realized, in her own spilled life's blood—upon the front of her robes. The bloody swaths began at her shoulders and met at a point between her breasts. It was a yoke of blood.

A slow apprehension was nagging at the back of the novice's mind. A dim awareness of having seen these sanguine markings before. The stark contrast between the black robes and the bright living band of color at the collar…

Sturbridge smiled down at her, extending both hands to draw Antigone to her feet. Taking the novice's forearm, Sturbridge tenderly raised it to her lips and ran her tongue over the wicked slash of the open wound. It closed at its master's touch.

"This is usually the point in the ceremony when you would partake of the Blood of the Seven. It is a reminder of your Oath of Initiation into this noble order, a rejuvenation of that first fiery idealism. It is also the renewed pledge of dedication to the Pyramid that seals your promotion to the Second Circle of the Novitiate. Given the events that will likely be awaiting us tomorrow evening, such a pledge seems somehow out of place, almost inauthentic. We will improvise."

Sturbridge laid open her own wrist with one fingernail.

"I...I don't understand," Antigone stammered.

Sturbridge smiled. "If you can work a truthsaying and subdue an Astor—in a single evening, no less—you are a Novice of the First Circle no longer. I will put through the necessary paperwork tonight, when I return to the chantry. There will be time enough. What you have done here this evening will be part of the record of our people before any report the Astors might bring against you."

The blood was flowing freely now. Sturbridge stretched out her arm. "I will not abandon you, Antigone. Even if the Pyramid itself should fall upon you."

Hesitantly, Antigone took Sturbridge's arm in both hands and bent over it. "I don't know why you're doing this. Even now. *Especially* now. When everything seems to be teetering on the brink. You don't have to. To anyone else it could make no difference. A hollow and useless gesture. But not to me. Whatever else will come of this, I thank you. I am, as always, yours to command, Regentia." She drank.

Sturbridge stroked Antigone's hair gently, in time to the electric, ecstatic spurt of the blood flowing between them. If anything, she held the embrace too long, until her own awareness was no more than a dim flutter.

"My child," she crooned softly over and over again to herself, "my beautiful little girl."

Antigone sputtered and choked upon the sudden mouthful of stagnant icy water. She broke away, consumed in a fit of coughing. Doubled over.

Sturbridge slowly came back to herself. The flow of blood from her forearm had ceased entirely. Instead, the wound seeped a chill dark water. The pink puckered flesh around it had taken on an unmistakably bluish tinge. Self-consciously, she smoothed her sleeve down over it.

222 / Eric Griffin

She thought of Eva, of the ambassador, of her own little girl. Of all the children who had gone before them into that dark well. "It is time," she said aloud.

Antigone turned and took one hesitant step toward her regent. "Regentia, I..."

"I know, little one. But the night has grown long and you must fly now. It is not safe for you to return to the chantry. You are a dangerous fugitive. A dark thaumaturge. You understand this?" She smiled.

"Yes. But where will I go?" Antigone asked.

Sturbridge was quiet a long time. She started hard at Antigone, but her vision was haunted by shadows. She kept seeing, not her novice standing on that precarious perch, but another. Leaning far out over the Widow's Walk. Trying to pry from the city spread out below its secrets.

"You will go underground, to the Nosferatu, to Calebros. You will tell them I sent you and that they are to keep you safe, at all costs. You may tell them they will do this for the sake of the bones that lie beneath the regent's blood. They will not refuse you sanctuary."

"Sanctuary," Antigone laughed nervously, thinking of her own caged bird. What would become of him now? "I understand. I will go into exile and willingly, Regentia. But what of my charge? I cannot leave Mr. Felton in the hands of the Astors. And I can't very well take him...."

"An exceptional idea. He will go into hiding with you. It will give the Nosferatu something to debate about, and they do so love a good debate. Being bound to protect the very assassin whose blood they have been hunting these last nights. Yes, it is a dilemma worthy of them. Do not fear. The Nosferatu know the value of a bargain, a favor, a debt unpaid. They will keep the both of you safely enough. No more arguments now, and no long good-byes. It is better this way. The shadow of the

Pyramid is long enough—" she began the traditional words of leave-taking and then broke off.

"That one more might shelter beneath it," Antigone finished, realizing that, for the first time in seventy years, she would not be shielded by the protecting bulk of the Pyramid.

"In this case, far beneath it." Sturbridge smiled. "Good-bye, Antigone."

Antigone's voice was soft, subdued. "Good-bye, then." Slowly, she turned and began walking. She had no particular destination in mind, but her feet instinctively sought out the path of least resistance. The place that they were most comfortable. The very edge of the precipice.

She seemed to gain in confidence with each stride. There was now a hint of purpose in Antigone's measured step although her course remained exactly as before—picking her way silently and methodically along the very edge of the abyss.

The prince's mistake, she thought, was that he had forgotten about the catch platforms. Or perhaps he'd misjudged their reach. It was not enough to slip over the side, to merely step out into the arms of the abyss. These things required a certain boldness, a certain abandon.

Reaching the corner, she saw the lights of Broadway spread out below her like ships' lanterns swaying from the bows of boats tied up along a quayside. They flickered, bobbing in time to the lapping of unseen waves. There were sacred galleries hidden there, she knew. Pockets of air nestled just below the docks, silent chambers defined by the rows of tarred wooden pilings sunk into the seabed. She remembered them well. At night, diving beneath the chill waters and the crowding hulls of moored fishing boats, one might win through—break the surface *below* the docks, in the sacred chamber ringed with wooden obelisks. The pillars were carved with the names and signs of the faithful. There they might exchange secrets, or schemes, or covert kisses—in the darkness, shivering and treading water.

Antigone slipped from the cumbersome black robes, long the symbol of her novitiate, of her failure. The bloody badge of her final triumph over the forces of inertia was still fresh upon the breast. The coarse and awkward second skin she had worn these seventy years slipped to the scarred concrete. She stood poised upon the very edge of the precipice, naked and radiant in the moonlight. She breathed deeply of the cool night air. Her arms stretched upward as if she would catch the moon in the net of her outspread fingers. Her body arced, taut and youthful. Deceptively so. In that single unselfconscious gesture, it belied a century of memories and responsibilities.

Her body bounded high, flashed in the moonlight like a fish breaking the plane of the water and, for a moment, soaring. At the crux of the arc, she bent perfectly double, fingers touching toes and then unfolding sharply like a straight razor. Then she succumbed to the gentle tug of the earth. Calling her name, calling her home.

There was a rushing of wind in her ears, billowing her hair out and back. She dove through it, beating powerful strokes, trying to fight deep enough that she might win through—might make it all the way under the keels of the moored boats and emerge in the pillared recess beneath the docks, the sanctuary of the watery tomb.

At the foot of the Empire State Building, David Foucault, Channel 11 News, spilled his coffee, sputtered and nearly choked. "Jeezus! Look at that—Jack, grab that damned camera!" He wiped at the long, wet coffee stain that ran the entire length of his front. He leaned way over backward—as he had a moment before, trying to get at the last drop of tepid coffee—now craning up toward the observation deck.

"Where?" Jack challenged. He had been the brunt of Foucault's little jokes before.

David thrust an angry finger skyward, jabbing at the slight but unmistakable silhouette framed against the disc of the moon.

"Son of a bitch! How the hell did that idiot get up there?" Jack scrambled for the camera. In one single motion he popped the lens cap and thumbed the roll-tape. The focus whirred even before the rig settled to rest on his shoulder.

"Damned if I know. Stairwell's buried in rubble and I've seen the remains of that elevator car. You getting all this?" Foucault demanded. He looked around nervously. Already the initial pounce of discovery was giving way to a gentle apprehension. He was not a slow man, and the inevitable question of the point of impact and an understandable concern for his own safety were fighting their way to the fore.

"Not getting a damned thing yet," Jack grumbled, squinting through the eyepiece and trying to blink free the moon-shaped retinal after-image. "You still got a bead on him?"

"Listen!" Foucault's whisper was sharp, imperative. A low whistling rush of air bore down upon them. "Shit." He began scrambling hurriedly around the van, toward the shelter of buildings across the street. Jack held his ground a moment longer. Two. Three. Then broke away under his partner's barrage of profanities.

"All right, I'm coming." He bent low, nearly double, cradling the camera beneath his chest, as if he would rather take the blow on his head than on his footage. He braced against the imminent impact.

Nothing.

"Real funny, asshole." Having reached Foucault's bunker, the doorway of a shop opposite, Jack punched his partner ungently in the shoulder.

"What the hell?" Foucault said. He walked out from cover, scanning the skies as if for an expected downpour that had suddenly failed to materialize. A sudden breeze ruffled his hair, but the only feature he could pick out in the inscrutable face of the night sky was the outline of a solitary night bird pulling out of a long dive. Struggling for altitude. A piercing, mournful cry, and then gone.

About the Author

Eric Griffin is the author of the Tremere Trilogy (*Widow's Walk, Widow's Weeds, Widow's Might*) as well as *Tremere* and *Tzimisce* in the best-selling Clan Novel series. His short stories have appeared in the *CN:Anthology*. Other published works include *The Three Pillars* and *Castles and Covenants.*

He is currently co-developer of the Tribe Novel series for *Werewolf: the Apocalypse.*

Griffin was initiated into the bardic mysteries at their very source, Cork, Ireland. He is currently engaged in that most ancient of Irish literary traditions—that of the writer in exile. He resides in Atlanta, Georgia, with his lovely wife Victoria and his three sons, heroes-in-training all.

Curious about other Crossroad Press books? Stop by our
website: http://crossroadpress.com
We offer quality writing
in digital, audio, and print formats.

Subscribe to our newsletter on the website homepage and
receive a free eBook.